TACKETT

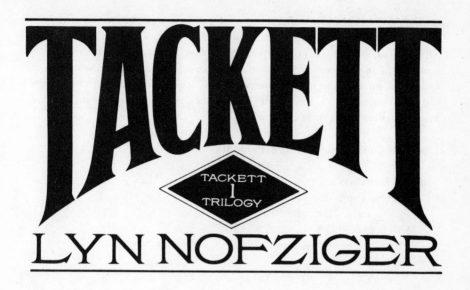

TACKETT

TACKETT
1
TRILOGY

LYN NOFZIGER

TUMBLEWEED PRESS
Washington, D.C.

Library of Congress Cataloging-in-Publication Data

Nofziger, Franklyn C.
    Tackett / Lyn Nofziger.
        p.   cm.—(Tackett trilogy ; 1)
    ISBN 0-89526-495-1
    I. Title.   II. Series: Nofziger, Franklyn C. Tackett trilogy ; 1.
PS3564.034T33   1993
813'.54—dc20   93-8244
                                                                                   CIP

Published in the United States by
Tumbleweed Press
an imprint of
Regnery Gateway
1130 17th Street, NW
Washington, DC 20036

Distributed to the trade by
National Book Network
4720-A Boston Way
Lanham, MD 20706

Printed on acid-free paper.

Manufactured in the United States of America.

10 9 8 7 6 5 4 3 2 1

In memory of Louis L'Amour,
the greatest Western writer of them all.

PREFACE

ONE DAY IN mid-1972 a man with a Texas accent walked into my office in Los Angeles and said words to the effect that "I have a way to help insure the re-election of the president."

That piqued my interest a bit since I was running Richard Nixon's re-election campaign in California, but really not all that much because in recent months I had had at least 77 visits and calls from other persons who also had the secret of victory at their fingertips.

"Pray, tell," I said. "And what may that be?"

"If President Nixon will have his picture taken with Louis L'Amour that will do it," my new friend said.

"And who, may I ask," I asked, "is Louis L'Amour?"

He looked at me aghast. What kind of ignoramus was I never to have heard of Louis (pronounced Louie) L'Amour. "He is the most famous Western writer in the world. He's sold over 20 million copies of his books."

Remember, this was in 1972. By the time he died in 1991 he'd sold more than a hundred million copies—not the Bible but not bad.

"Is he as good as Max Brand (of *Destry Rides Again* fame)?"

"Better," he said.

"And he wants to endorse Nixon?"

Well, it turned out, not exactly. The great man never endorsed politicians but he would have his picture taken with Nixon, and that in itself would send a message to all 20 million L'Amour readers.

vii

"Well," I said, "I don't think we can work that out unless he endorses."

He took my turndown graciously even though he allowed as how I was making a mistake. Regardless, he left with me two paperback books by Mr. L'Amour, *The Broken Gun*, a contemporary Western, and *The Day Breakers*, an early novel in a series L'Amour had written and would continue to write about "The magnificent Sackett family." A few days later my new friend called and invited me to have lunch with him and Louis and Kathy L'Amour and, it turned out, a couple of other people whose names I have long since forgotten. Lunch, as it was every other time I ate with Louis L'Amour, was in the dining room of the Beverly Hills Hotel where the author had his own special table.

He was a big man, husky without being fat, soft-spoken and pleasant. He dressed like a Westerner. His wife was dark-haired and beautiful. She still is. She is also very nice.

The lunch was good—he bought—but not remarkable and afterward I went back to running the campaign. I set his books aside—campaigns can be all-consuming—and thought no more about them until after the election. Then I picked them up, one at a time, and read them. Not bad. In fact, pretty good. Growing up I had read western pulp fiction and western books by authors such as Zane Grey, Will James, Owen Wister and my favorite, Max Brand. Louis L'Amour had them all beaten.

But it wasn't until early December that I really discovered Louis L'Amour. We had driven to Death Valley because I wanted to go to some place hot. The old hotel there is a wonderful place, the food is good, our room had a fireplace, and there is a little shop that doesn't sell much of anything but at that time did have a rack of paperback books including 13 by Louis L'Amour. Which was lucky because it was brutally cold outside and windy. I read those 13 books in the six days we were there. Since then I have read them all at least one more time as well as everything else I could find published under Louis L'Amour's name, even a book of his poetry.

For years Bantam put out two a year. For years I read the two new

ones and several old ones. I still reread a few each year. For the
most part they're short; they don't take long.

Finally, a couple of years ago, I woke up one day and said to
myself, "I think I will write a novel after the manner of Louis
L'Amour." So I did.

I named my hero Del Tackett, easily and deliberately to let the
other characters in the novel confuse him with Tell Sackett, one of
the magnificent gunfighting Sacketts from the hills of Tennessee.
Tackett, who grew up in a high Sierras mining camp, is as big and
tough and uncurried as any Sackett. Like every Sackett he, too, is a
knight errant in western garb, a loner and a rover.

Most of the time, however, I don't know where he's roving or
what he's thinking until he takes control of my fingers on the word
processor. I am, I have decided, not so much his creator as I am his
chronicler.

Wherever Louis L'Amour has gone I hope one day he meets Del
Tackett and I hope even more fervently that these two genuine he-
men—one real, one fictional— will like each other. Because if it
weren't for Louis L'Amour Tackett would not exist, not now or ever,
even in my imagination, and he had damn well better realize it.

And finally, one last word to Kathy L'Amour, and to the children, Beau and Angelica. I hope you will like Del Tackett, too. In
his own blunt, sometimes bumbling and totally unconscious way,
he follows as best he can the examples laid down by the Sacketts of
honesty, loyalty, self-reliance, and gentleness, toward women and
children. Because he is who he is and what he is I have dedicated
him as a sincere tribute to your husband and father.

Lyn Nofziger

TACKETT

CHAPTER 1

I WAS STANDING there at the bar of a run-down saloon in this cow-town along the New Mexico-Arizona border. It was called Nora after an enterprising lady who had seen a need in this part of the country and had come in some years before with six girls and a covered wagon hoping to meet it.

I was nursing a drink and minding my business when a gnarled old man came in. He was dusty and had only one arm, but he had sharp gray eyes and a six-gun hanging on his hip on the side where he had an arm. He kind of sidled up to me and looked longingly at my drink.

"Pour yerself one," I said indicating the bottle at my elbow.

The skinny bartender slid him a glass and he poured himself a tall one and downed it in a single gulp. He sighed and wiped his mouth with the back of his hand.

"Dry," he said. "Been ridin' since dawn." Then he changed the subject.

"You Tackett?" he asked.

I'm the taciturn type. I nodded.

"Thought so," he said. "Wanna thank ya now fer the drink. Probly the last un you'll buy me."

"Have another," I said. "But first tell me what yer drivin' at."

He poured his drink but let it sit. "Feller named Sears waitin' out there in the street. Says to tell you if you come out he'll kill ya. Says if you run or hide he'll find ya. Says ya might as well come on out now."

Now I'm not a swearing man but I swore now. "Shee-ut," I said softly, glad there wasn't no ladies around to hear me. Up there in that Sierra Nevada gold camp where I grew up Ma had made it plain she didn't believe much in swearing or vulgarity. Funny, too, because when she was out there panning for gold with the best of them she heard enough of it from those rough-hewn men all around her. Maybe that's what turned her off.

I didn't know that man waiting out there in that dusty street, but I sure knew who he was. He was Jack Sears, a Nevada mining camp gunman. I had killed his brother and his father and a cousin when they tried to highjack a load of gold I was guarding on its way down from the mountains into Carson City.

They had come up out of the rocks along the trail and shot the wagon driver in cold blood. They didn't see me lying in the wagon bed sheltered by sacks of gold ore. They'd hardly pulled their triggers when I let loose with a volley from the Winchester in my hands. I got the old man and the cousin dead center with my first two shots and winged the brother as he wheeled his horse and tore out of there. I found him five miles down the trail where he'd fallen off his horse and bled to death from a wound that looked like it had nicked one of them big arteries.

I tossed him in the wagon with the gold and his father and his cousin. I recognized all three of them. They'd been hanging around the mines up there in the Sierra with no visible means of support and a reputation for being hard cases.

Jack Sears wasn't no better than them, but when they tried that robbery he'd been laid up with a busted leg—happened when his horse shied at a rattlesnake and threw him. They didn't get him word of the shooting until two or three days afterward and by that time I'd drifted.

I was sick of the gold fields and the violence that was so much a part of them. I'd left them before, when I was sixteen and ma told me I was old enough to go it on my own. For the next twelve years I'd herded cows, fought a few Indians down along the border, ridden shotgun on a stage or two, and just generally drifted around the west, always looking for some place to light and never quite finding it. I'd gone back to Lodestone, the little mining camp where ma had panned gold all those years, because a wandering cowhand come across me in Utah and passed on the word that she was dead.

I cussed out loud that time and taken off for Lodestone without waiting to draw my pay from the stage line I was riding shotgun for. I got to Lodestone and found her grave in the little cemetery they'd carved out of the slope above the town. Someone had been good enough to put a wooden cross over it and had written on it

MA TACKETT, DIED 1888

Just Ma Tackett. Nobody knowed her first name, not even me. She'd always been just plain Ma Tackett to everybody she knew, and that was about everybody in the camp. She'd befriended half of them. Lent 'em a buck for a meal or taken care of 'em when they were sick. But she never talked much about herself. She'd come into Lodestone when the camp was new, walking up from the direction of Carson City, leading a burro packed with all her belongings and carrying a six-year-old boy on its back—me.

We'd been down in Carson City ever since I could remember, with Ma working as a waitress, but we left late one night on mighty short notice and headed for the hills with nothing but the clothes on our backs and what that old burro could carry.

When I was growing up I heard rumors every now and then that Ma had killed a man down there in Carson City, a man who couldn't take "no" for an answer until in trying to fight him off one night she bashed him with a handy chunk of rock. Turned out he had a thin-boned skull. He also had friends, so Ma up and left.

I never ever knew my Pa. Ma never spoke of him and never wore a wedding ring. When I was old enough to figure it out I figured Ma had made one of those mistakes that even nice girls make now and then and I was the fallout from it.

Maybe that was why, all the time I was growing up Ma never had much use for men. Leastwise she never had anyone you could call her sweetheart or her man. Too bad, too. She'd been a handsome woman. Big and rawboned and strong and with a fine featured face and figure to match. But over the years she got weatherbeaten from working along the creeks, her waist had thickened from all the stooping and lifting and her hands had gotten as rough and calloused as any miner's.

But she was my ma and I loved her, and though I hadn't seen her for twelve years I'd sent word to her every year or two, and a couple of her letters had even found their way to me. So I wasn't ashamed that in looking at that rude cross I shed a tear before heading down to the town to see what I could find out.

Wasn't many folks left in Lodestone I'd known as a boy but old Horace Dealy was still running his general store and acting as agent for the stage line. Turned out he'd taken care of Ma's burying and had put the cross up with the writing on it. Turned out that Ma'd died of pneumonia and there wasn't no doctor in Lodestone to treat her, not that he could have done much good. Folks get pneumonia they either make it or they don't. Ma didn't.

Ma didn't leave much in the way of worldly goods. She'd lived in a two-room shack all them years and it stood deserted now. She'd made enough money panning gold so she got by, but she never had anything left over. Old man Dealy had gone through the shack and the only thing he found that he thought he ought to hold for me if I ever came back was an old leather-bound diary. He had never got around to looking through it; maybe he figured it was none of his business. When I showed up he gave it to me and I shoved it in my saddlebag, meaning to look at it later. Then I forgot all about it.

Turned out also that old man Dealy was in charge of a shipment of gold to Carson. He had a driver but he needed someone to guard that gold. Them Searses had been hanging around town for three or four weeks and Dealy had a hunch they wasn't there for honest reasons. He'd seen the gun on my hip, noticed it looked like it had been used a time or two, and offered me the job.

I told him I'd take it but I didn't want anyone to know. We'd leave before dawn with me snuggled down behind those sacks of ore. We figured anybody tried to stop that wagon I'd get the drop on them and take them on down to Carson where they could try them and put them in prison. We didn't figure they'd just up and cut down on Hughey Newton, who was driving the wagon. He was a harmless galoot and everybody knowed it. Didn't even pack a gun.

So I'd done what I had to do, gunned them down with the same amount of mercy they showed Newton. And now, because I'd done what I had to do, the last of the Searses and the toughest one of the lot was out there in the middle of the road waiting for me. I was tired of violence, tired of killing. If I'd been tinhorn enough to carve notches on my gun I'd have had five of them, not counting the Sears clan, and I didn't want any more. I thought for a moment of going out the back door but then I knew it wouldn't do any good. Jack Sears, big and tough and utterly ruthless, would track me down wherever I went. So I might as well get it over with now.

I taken a deep breath, hitched my gun around in front a little, and started for the door. That saloon was suddenly as quiet as the dawn before the rooster crows. Folks there figured I was going outside and wasn't never coming back in. Me, I figured different. I didn't want to kill Jack Sears but I was going to if I had to, even if he killed me, too.

I might not be the fastest draw in the West but I was fast enough to get a shot in and careful enough to make my first shot count. Too many trigger-happy gunmen paid too much attention to speed and not enough to accuracy. Most of them died pretty young. Jack Sears wasn't no boy but I didn't think he'd ever run into anyone who'd really been up the creek and over the mountain the way I'd been. Anyway, I'd soon find out.

Of a sudden I stopped. If I walked out into that bright sunshine from the dim light of the saloon I'd be half-blind for a few seconds, but long enough for him to see me and go for his gun before I could even see where he was at.

I turned and went out the back door. Wasn't no alley back there, just sagebrush in the distance. I waited a few seconds until I could see good, then I walked quietly around the side of the building. When I reached the front corner I saw this big galoot standing in the middle of the street, staring at the saloon doors.

"You lookin' for me, Sears?" I said loud enough for him to hear, as I continued to walk toward him. He swung around at the sound of my voice, but he didn't go for his gun. He was wearing two of them, tied down low, and was wearing black jeans, a black shirt, and a black hat, like he wanted folks to know he was a bad apple.

"You're Tackett," he said. "Ain't you? Well, I'm gonna kill you and feed you to the buzzards."

He was one of those people who like to talk before they fight. Don't mean they're cowards. It's just their way of doing things. Me, I kept on walking toward him.

"We'll see," I said, as I drew closer.

Suddenly, he took another look at me. He couldn't figure me out. He'd expected me to stop in the street and then, kind of by mutual consent, we'd both go for our guns. But I'd just kept walking and now I was just a few feet from him. All at once he went almost frantically for his gun. But I was too close to him now, and I fetched him a short right hand with all my two hundred pounds behind it right along his jaw. His gun never even cleared leather as he sprawled backwards into the dust. His hand went clawing for his gun again but I taken one long step and stomped on it, grinding it into the dirt with my boot heel. He screamed, but I paid him no mind. Instead, I reached down and hauled him to his feet by the front of his black shirt.

Then I slapped him and backhanded him three or four times across the face, all the time holding him by the front of that black shirt. Then I turned him around, grabbed him by the collar and the seat of his black jeans, and tiptoed him over to the watering trough and shoved him in. He come up sputtering and I reached out and put my big, old, calloused hand on top of his head and shoved him down under again. I held him there for about thirty seconds before I let him come up.

He crawled to his feet and stood there in the middle of that watering trough, holding his busted right hand against his chest and kind of whimpering.

"Sears," I said, "you are big and you are mean, but you ain't tough. Now you get out of this town and don't never show me your face again because the next time I see you you'll wish I'd killed you this time."

I turned my back on him, and someone in the crowd that had gathered handed me my hat, and I headed back for the saloon. I wasn't much of a drinking man but I hadn't even finished the one I was nursing when the one-armed oldster brought me word that Sears was waiting. He was still leaning on the bar when I shoved my way back inside.

"Heerd you give that feller a beatin'," he said.

I turned on him. "Who are you and what do you want? You didn't come here just to tell me Sears was out there waitin'."

"Nope," he said. "Boss said to find you. Wants to talk to you."

I was silent for a minute. I'd only been in Nora for three days and had spent that time minding my own business and I didn't recall seeing anyone I knew. He sensed my puzzlement.

"Cowboy ridin' the grub line come by couple of days ago. Mentioned he'd seen ya here. Said he'd seen ya in action over near Globe. Said you was a good hand with a gun."

Globe. That was two years back. I'd caught a man cheating in a poker game and when I mentioned it to him he went for his gun. I'd shoved the table over on top of him, kicked his gun away, and given him a beating. He found me the next night in a saloon and pulled his gun when my back was turned. But I seen him in the mirror behind the bar, ducked to one side, pulled out my own gun and shot him dead.

He was the fourth man I'd killed and I wasn't happy about it, getting a reputation as a gunfighter and all. So I drifted out of there and wound up punching cows near San Bernardino for a year, but they were beginning to plant orange trees there and I couldn't take the smell of the blossoms. Made me sneeze. So I hit the trail again.

Over at Las Vegas a kid who thought he was good with a gun picked a fight with me but wouldn't come close enough for me to tackle with my hands. When he drawed on me he didn't leave me much choice, even though I surely didn't want to kill him. I lit out again, hoping to find that place where I could settle down. Maybe start a little ranch. Maybe find the right girl to spend the rest of my life with. One thing for sure, I wanted to go somewhere where my reputation hadn't caught up with me, which is why I headed out for Salt Lake City. Taken me just a few weeks, though, to decide their ways weren't my ways—all I wanted was one wife—and I was about ready to move on when the news came of Ma's death.

"Who ya ridin' for?" I asked, taking a sip of my whiskey.

"The R Bar R," he said. "Over up against the mountains."

"I'm job huntin'," I said. "I'll punch cows or drive stage or ride shotgun but I don't hire out for gunfightin'."

"It's punchin' cows," he said. "Only thing is, we're a couple of hands shy and there's some rustlin' been goin' on. Couple of the boys got scared and left and the boss is lookin' for someone who don't scare."

I chewed on that for a minute, then shrugged my shoulders. What the heck, the job was punching cows. If there was trouble with rustlers, well, that was part of the job. It wasn't no range war or anything like that where they'd be hiring my gun. At least I told myself that was the case.

"Ain't had me no lunch," I said. "Let's get a bite and then we'll go see your boss."

The R Bar R was close to twenty miles north and east of Nora, up against the mountains and close to the continental divide. Everything west of there, which the R Bar R was, flows over toward the Colorado River and eventually down to the Gulf of California. East of the divide everything flows either to Rio Grande or over to the Missouri and Mississippi.

Nora, sitting on the edge of the Painted Desert the way it did, was pretty dry. A creek ran through it in the rainy seasons. Otherwise folks had wells. Funny thing, with all that dry land you didn't have to dig very deep to find water. The old madam who'd started the town, her full name was Nora Wetstone, had not only found water, but she'd planted some cottonwood trees around the adobe house she'd hired some Mexicans to build for her. Between the trees and the thick adobe walls the place was cool even on the hottest days, which maybe accounted for some of her summertime business.

It turned out the one-armed puncher's name was Billy Bob Doyle. It was a name I'd heard of. He'd been a Texas Ranger once and a no-nonsense cow-town marshal in a couple of places. Over lunch he told me how he'd lost his arm.

"I wasn't being no hero," he said. "There was half a dozen drunken cowboys raisin' hell and I went to quiet 'em down and one of 'em took a shot at me. Hit me in the arm. Didn't seem serious but it got infected. The doc said blood poisonin'. Told me I could take my choice—lose my arm or my life. I let him take my arm. Had to learn to shoot left-handed."

We didn't do much talking on the ride to the ranch. Billy Bob had come to town in a wagon so he could pick up some supplies, too. So I tied my horse to the wagon and rode along with him. It was a long ride but we were both pretty quiet during most of it. I thought some about Ma and wished I'd got back to Lodestone to see her afore she died. Maybe by now she'd have been ready to talk some about my pa, who he was, where we was from and were they married. I'd always hoped Ma had been married. I'd loved her dearly, but, still, having her married would have made me feel better.

When I wasn't thinking about Ma I spent some time kind of patting myself on the back for not shooting it out with Jack Sears. I didn't want to be known as a gunman and I sure wasn't eager to add to the list of men I'd shot. But, still, I'd known I had to face up to Sears somehow and doing it with my fists instead of my gun made me feel good. I'd never gotten the urge to kill just for the sake of killing, like some of the hotshot gunmen around, and now I was pretty sure I'd never get it.

We pulled into the ranch yard along about sundown and this big black dog come bounding off the porch to greet us. I stepped back not liking the idea of serving as dog food, but she kind of sidled up to me and rubbed against my leg. I reached down to pat her and she licked my hand. Billy Bob called her off and she tailwagged her way over to him.

"Name is Black Beauty," he said. "We call her Beauty. Sweetest dog you ever saw and the worst watchdog. Even likes Injuns. But the boss likes her. Raised her from a pup.

"When you get yer horse taken care of come on up to the house. We all eat in the kitchen."

By that time I'd gotten the horses unhitched and turned into the corral. I taken my own horse off to the barn, unsaddled him, and rubbed him down a bit with a handful of hay. I left him in a stall eating his dinner and went up to the house hoping to get some of my own. It was a big house, built of adobe except for the wooden veranda that stretched the width of the house. And I noticed when riding up that the yard was neat, none of the junk you find lying around a lot of ranches, and there was even some red flowers planted up against the veranda and along the path leading to the steps. Thought crossed my mind that there was a woman's hand at work there, probably the rancher's wife.

I went around to the back door where I saw a pan of water and a piece of towel on a nail so I rinsed off my face and hands, dried them, and knocked. I heard Billy Bob holler to me to come in and just then the door opened and this girl was standing there. The last rays of the setting sun lighted her up and kind of glittered off of her black hair. Her face was just short of beautiful, oval-shaped, with a wide mouth, lips meant for kissing, a straight nose, and eyes about as black as her hair. My shadow kind of obscured her figure but I could see enough shape to know I wanted to see more.

"Won't you come in, Mr. Tackett," she said in a soft, warm voice that I could see now matched her figure. I went on in, having to brush by her as I went, and she smelled clean and fresh, a lot different from them perfumed girls at Nora's and some other places I'd been. Different from Ma, too, who'd always smelled of hard work. There in the light I got a good look at her without appearing to stare. She was one of those kind of round women, not chubby but not skinny, neither. She was about five foot four with a small waist and nicely filled out both above it and below.

While I was taking that quick look at her she had a chance to size me up, too. Wasn't much to look at. Oh, I'm big enough. About six foot two with my boots on and weigh around two hundred pounds, most of it my chest and shoulders which comes from all the digging and other hard work I did as a kid around Lodestone. Fact is, from the time I was big enough to hold a pick and shovel I'd been doing nothing but hard work with my arms and back instead of with my brains. That kind of life don't do nothing but build muscle in both your body and your head.

I must of looked kind of tough, too. I needed a haircut and a shave and I had this three-inch scar across my left cheek where a fast and mean Mexican had nicked me in a knife fight down El Paso way. Last I seen of the Mexican his friends was carrying him off, bleeding like a stuck pig. I heard later he'd recovered, though, and I was glad. Like I said, I don't enjoy killing.

I was wearing a pair of black jeans that needed washing and a checkered shirt that wasn't much cleaner, and one gun hanging low on my right thigh and tied down. There was a thong over the butt to keep it in the holster whilst I was riding. I was holding a black, flatcrowned hat which I hung on a hook by the door.

She took me in in one quick glance and then said, "Welcome to the R Bar R, Mr. Tackett. I am Esmeralda Rankin. I am the owner of the R Bar R."

I guess I did another double take—I sure wasn't expecting to work for no woman, not that I got anything against women, only I just didn't expect to run into one running a ranch in the middle of nowhere—because she smiled, showing even white teeth, then went on:

"My father came to this country about 10 years ago and built this ranch. He was killed last year out on the range. His horse dragged him."

She turned to where Billy Bob and another cowboy were sitting at a kitchen table hugging mugs of coffee. "You know Billy Bob. And this is Evan Stevens."

Stevens gave me a quick, hard stare, then nodded. He was a sandy-haired man with a square face that burned instead of tanning. He had washed-out gray eyes and a thin-lipped mouth that looked like it had never smiled.

She turned to go back to the stove, and as she turned I could see a tear forming in the corner of her eye. Couldn't say as I blamed her, having her pa killed like that and leaving her alone to run a ranch out in the middle of nowhere. It wasn't much of a life for a lone woman, especially one who was young and pretty, what with rustlers around and being short-handed and all.

I grabbed a chair and sat down across the big table from Billy Bob and Evan Stevens. Billy Bob sat there grinning at me like he couldn't quit and I knew he figured he'd put one over on me, not telling me he worked for a woman. Probably figured I wouldn't have come if I'd of knowed it. The table was big enough to seat ten or twelve people and probably had come close to that at one time. I taken a minute to look around the room. There was Beauty asleep and snoring gently over in the corner, but the thing I noticed most was a sink with a pump right next to it. Old man Rankin must have dug a well and built the house over it. It not only made things convenient but it also made the house easier to defend. That was a pretty cagy old man, I thought.

Esmeralda began putting heaping plates of food on the table and when she sat down we all dug in. It was plain food, but well seasoned and good. The beef was tender, the beans was Mex-Tex hot which is how I like them, and there was thick baking powder biscuits with butter and wild honey Billy Bob had picked up in Nora. When we'd finished that up she brought over a fresh-baked apple pie and a big pot of steaming hot coffee. And that pie was good, real good. I didn't recollect having anything like it since I left home and Ma 12 years earlier.

After we finished up the pie and had a couple of mugs of coffee, I just leaned back in my chair and give a big, old contented sigh. I hadn't spent much time in warm, comfortable homes like this, nor eaten really good home cooking since I left the gold country.

After Esmeralda finished clearing the table she turned to Billy Bob and Evan Stevens and said, "If you boys don't mind I'd like to speak to Mr. Tackett alone."

They got up and went out but I noticed Stevens didn't look real happy about going. I noticed, too, that standing up he was almost as big as I am and he moved like a cat. He wasn't wearing no gun but he looked like if he had one he'd know what to do with it.

Esmeralda must have seen his look, too, because after they'd gone she said, "Don't mind Evan, Mr. Tackett. He looks on himself as my guardian—at least."

She smiled a little smile when she said it and then came right to the point. "I'd like to hire you, Mr. Tackett. I need another man here. In fact, I really need three more men. This is a big range and it takes half a dozen men to work it properly. But after Father was killed, rustlers began moving on us. They shot at two of our men, not meaning to hit them, just frighten them, and they succeeded. They both quit and for the last two weeks there's just been the three of us trying to hold the cattle in close. But we're too spread out for us to do what has to be done. And in the meantime I know we're losing cattle."

"Miss Esmeralda," I said. "I come out here plannin' on hirin' on, but you got to understand, I want to hire on to punch cows, not to do no gun fightin'. But you got to know somethin' else, too. I ride for the brand and I'll do what has to be done so long as I'm ridin' for you, and if that means fightin' rustlers, well, that's the way it's gonna be."

"Thank you, Mr. Tackett," she said.

"One more thing, Miss Esmeralda," I said. "You can call me

Del. My real name is William Delligan Tackett, but you can call me Del."

"Tackett," she mused. "Del Tackett. Wasn't there a gunfighter up around Mora with a name something like that?"

"I wouldn't know, Ma'am," I said. "I ain't never been up that way."

She rose to signify the meeting was over but as I started out the door she stopped me. "One more thing Mr. Tackett—Del—I want you to be my foreman, but please don't say anything to the boys tonight. I'll tell them at breakfast."

I strolled over to the adobe bunkhouse, picked up my bedroll which I'd set by the door, and went in. Billy Bob was reading an old magazine by lantern light and Evan Stevens was playing solitaire with a dirty pack of cards. Billy Bob looked up.

"Hire on?" he asked.

"Yeah," I replied, throwing my bedroll on an empty bunk.

Stevens spoke without looking up from his cards. "Now we'll see if you're as tough as your reputation," he said with just the touch of a sneer in his voice.

"I'm just as tough as I have to be," I said. "Don't make me prove it."

I changed the subject before he could say anything back. "Boss lady wants to see us bright and early, so I'm turnin' in."

I hung my gun belt on a chair beside the bed and stuck my Colt .45 under my pillow. Then I shucked my boots and, pulling up my right pant leg, I unstrapped a sheath that was holding a knife with a six-inch blade sharp enough to shave by. I shoved it between my bedroll and the mattress, taken off my jeans, and crawled between the blankets.

Tomorrow, somehow, some way, I was going to find the time and place to take a bath. Last Saturday seemed a long time ago. Truth was, I didn't want to have that pretty girl up in the big ranch house think I was a pig. Besides, I'd noticed that Stevens, while he might have been surly, was clean and neat. Least I could do was be clean and neat, too, if I was going to ramrod this outfit.

CHAPTER 2

I WAS UP in the morning with the first light. Pulling on my pants and boots I went outside, found a bucket and pumped it full of water. I poured part of it into a dented tin basin that sat on the bench by the bunkhouse door along with a sliver of homemade lye soap. Using that I washed my face and hands and arms and chest. I fished my razor out of my saddlebag and stropped it a mite on the side of my boot. After I soaped up my face I began hacking at three days growth of beard. I hadn't no mirror but I was used to that and I done a pretty good job without nicking me even once.

When I finished I dragged my other shirt out and put it on. A couple of days ago I had paid one of Nora's girls two dollars to wash it and my other set of underwear. Easiest two dollars she was going to make that day even though it meant bending over a washboard. I thought back to her for a minute. She was young, probably not yet twenty, blond and pretty in a wholesome sort of way. Didn't look the kind to be working for Nora, but a girl alone in a man's world has to do something to earn a living. I'd known of more than one girl who got into that business because she had no choice, then latched on to some cowboy or rancher and made him a good wife. I kind of shrugged. A man might do worse.

By now smoke was rising from the kitchen chimney so I headed up to the house. I'd heard Billy Bob and Stevens stirring in the bunkhouse and knew they wouldn't be far behind. I knocked and went on in.

There was bacon frying on the stove, and she was standing by it mixing some batter that I took to be either hotcakes or biscuits.

17

"Mornin', Miss Esmeralda," I said.

She picked up a coffeepot and came over to the table which she'd already set for the four of us, and poured me a cup of hot, black coffee. It tasted good, and if that cold water I'd washed in hadn't got me wide awake a couple of sips of her coffee would have done the trick.

"Good morning, Del," she said. "And please, call me Esme. Esmeralda is a pretty name but it's much too long. Besides, Father always called me Esme."

"I ain't your father, Miss Esmeralda," I said. "But if it don't sound too forward I'd be plumb honored to call you Esme."

Just then the door open and Stevens came in, followed by Billy Bob.

They both grunted a "good morning" and sat down at the table. Esme came over and poured them coffee and went back to flipping flapjacks. I noticed Stevens followed her with his eyes and if looks mean anything it was clear to me he would have liked to do more than just look.

I had a chance to look around the room in the daylight. It was a big room, big enough for the table which could seat eight easy, the big cook stove with a wood box on one side of it, a dry sink on the other side, and next to it the porcelain wet sink I'd noticed last night sitting where you could pump water into it. Wasn't often you saw something like that back here. I figured the old colonel must have had it shipped in from Kansas City or maybe the other direction from San Franciso.

The adobe walls were whitewashed and I'd noticed when I came in they must have been a couple of feet thick. There was a window on the east side and another on the south wall, and both had heavy wood shutters you could swing shut and lock with a wooden bar. The ceiling consisted of wide planks laid over three heavy hand-hewn beams while the floor was a Mexican tile that he probably had freighted up from Santa Fe or El Paso. There was a trapdoor in the ceiling, and I figured the old colonel had decided if he was attacked by Indians it would be easier to fight them off from the roof. I'd noticed the outside walls were several feet higher than the inside ceiling which meant that a few armed men up on the roof could fight off an attack from all four directions.

About the time I'd finished looking the place over Esme began dishing up the bacon and hotcakes. There was more of that butter and honey Billy Bob had fetched from Nora and we dug right in. Beauty got up from where she'd been sleeping in the corner and ambled over hoping for a bite. I slipped her a bit of bacon and a minute later a piece of hotcake. After she'd finished that she lay down beside my chair and went back to sleep.

I looked over at Esme and she was kind of smiling, like she seen what I was doing. Some folks don't like feeding a dog at the table, but I always figured if I owned a dog I'd want it to be part of the family. Esme was even prettier with the sun streaming in through the east window than she had been last night. I saw now there were tints of red in her near-black hair. She had a short, straight nose with just the hint of a hump in it and chin that was firm without being prominent. Her eyes in the daylight were a dark blue. She was wearing a red-and-blue gingham dress that didn't do much to hide her shape. If she was self-conscious about being pretty and womanly among a bunch of rough cowhands she didn't show it. I suspect she was used to them and used to being looked at. And it was clear that even though she was doing the cooking she knew who the boss was—her.

We'd finished breakfast and were on our third mugs of coffee when Esme spoke up. There was no hemming and hawing with that woman. She came right to the point.

"I've asked Mr. Tackett to be foreman and take over the running of the ranch. He will report to me but from now on I want you boys to take your orders from him."

I heard Billy Bob say, "Fine by me." But I was watching Evan Stevens and he looked like he was about to cloud up and rain.

"Your father wanted me to be the foreman. He told me so before he was killed," he almost snarled, his red face even redder.

Esme replied calmly, "My father is dead. I am in charge now and I have decided that Mr. Tackett will be my foreman."

Stevens turned and glared at me. "I've been working here for two years and that job is mine by rights."

"I work for Miss Esme," I said, looking him in the eye. "And I take my orders from her."

He looked back at Esme. "You'll regret this," he said nastily. "I'm leaving and you can't run this ranch or hold it against the rustlers with a one-armed old man and a two-bit gunman. And that's all you've got because I'm quitting."

He stood up suddenly, shoving his chair back so hard it fell over backward, and slammed out the kitchen door.

Esme looked at me, her face white. "He's right. We can't run this ranch with just two men, much less fend off the rustlers. We couldn't do it if Evan had stayed. We just have to have two or three more men who aren't afraid to fight.

"Father borrowed money against the ranch to buy some good breeding stock and we're going to have to sell off some steers this fall to pay the mortgage, if I have any left to sell."

We talked a little bit about the ranch. She estimated she had about 3,500 head of cattle, most of them back up against the mountains, but she had no idea what the rustlers had stolen. All she knew was that Stevens had begun reporting a couple of months back that there were signs of cattle being drifted out of the country to the north, then someone had begun taking shots at all four of the hands when they were riding alone. Just last week two of them had quit, leaving only Stevens and Bill Bob Doyle. When the drifter had told her he'd seen me in Nora she sent Billy Bob in to see if she could hire me.

We were just winding up the conversation when we heard the pounding of hoofs slowly fade in the distance.

"There goes Stevens," Billy Bob said. "Just as well. Never cottoned to him nohow. Kind of a surly son of a gun and always eyein' Miss Esme."

Esme colored a little and said, "That doesn't matter. He was a good hand and we needed him."

"Miss Esme," I said. "I tell you what. I want you and Billy Bob to stay close to the ranch for the next couple of days. I'm going in to Nora and see if I can't round up a couple of hands. There were some fellers hangin' around there, didn't look like they was workin', and maybe by now they've drunk up the last of their wages."

I got up and headed for the door motioning Billy Bob to follow me. Outside I headed to the barn to saddle Old Dobbin, the bay gelding I had rode in on. I called him Old Dobbin because I'd won him in a poker game down in Globe off a rancher named Shay. I had kind of unhitched Old Dobbin from Shay, or so I decided.

Whilst I was saddling Old Dobbin I gave Billy Bob his instructions. "Stay close to the ranch while I'm gone. I may be gone two or three days and I don't like the idea of Miss Esme being here alone. Stevens has a real burr under his saddle and I don't know what he'll do. He's a dangerous man and if he comes back I want you around. And you can't tell about them rustlers. If they think there's a woman here alone they might take it in their minds to try to take over the ranch. In that case, if you can't stand 'em off you'll have to try to get her out of here. I'll be back as soon as I can."

I mounted Old Dobbin and touched him lightly with a spur and he was off like a shot. He'd had it pretty easy for a few days and he was raring to go. It wasn't yet noon when I cantered into Nora. I'd done me some thinking along the way. About halfway to Nora I'd begun kicking myself for not bringing Esme with me. The hotel in Nora wasn't much but she'd have been safer there than at the R Bar R, or so I thought.

I'd also got to thinking that Esme needed some company out there. It had to get mighty lonesome sometimes what with the hands out on the range and her there alone. Another person there would take some of the burden off of her as well as give her company. Besides, I knew it would make me ride easier if there was someone else there. It was something to think about and I had me an idea, if it could just work out.

First thing to do was to see if I could hire a man or two. So I headed for the Rocking Horse which was the other saloon in town. I lucked out. There was a couple of what looked to be punchers sitting at one of the tables drinking coffee. They didn't look exactly down on their luck but they didn't look flush, either. I moseyed up to the bar.

"Beer," I said, tossing a two-bit piece on the counter. The fat, bald bartender uncapped a bottle and set it in front of me. I was dry from the ride and I taken a big swig. Deliberately speaking loud, I asked him, "Know anyone around here looking for work? I need a couple of hands."

"You might ask those fellers over there," the bartender suggested. "They been loafin' around a few days. Don't seem to be workin'. Don't seem to be lookin' for work, either."

I heard a chair scrape and then the sound of boots headed my way. A voice asked, "You hirin', mister?"

"Could be," I said. "You lookin?"

I turned to look at him. He was lean and sandy haired. He had an open face with a mouth ready to smile and laughter crinkles around his eyes. He looked to be in his early twenties.

"Kind of," he said. "My pardner and me was punchin' cows down near El Paso but we decided it was time to see more country so we drawed our pay and drifted. We're runnin' a little low on money and we was just talkin' about huntin' us up a job. Only thing is, where one of us goes both of us go or it's no deal."

"Let's talk," I said. "Grab a beer for you and your buddy and come on over to the table."

I taken my beer and walked over to where his partner was waiting, pulled out a chair and sat down. They were about of a size only his partner was darker complected and had dark wavy hair. Might have been Mexican or part Indian.

"Name is Tackett," I said. "I'm ramroddin' the R Bar R north of

22

here up against the mountains. We're short-handed, we got troubles, and I'm huntin' help."

The dark-haired puncher kind of raised his eyebrows when he heard my name but it didn't seem to ring a bell with the blond one. Instead he took a swallow of his beer, wiped his mouth with his sleeve, and nodded his head toward his pardner. "He's Blackie Harrington. I'm Lew Haight."

Harrington took another look at me. "Knew of a prizefighter down around Beeville named Tackett or Hackett, somethin' like that. Watched him fight once. Wasn't as tall as you but bigger in the chest and shoulders. Packed a wallop like a mule. Knocked out that Tennessee fighter, Dunc Affrey, in fourteen rounds."

I was just a little bit irritated. I was tired of being mistook for someone else. "Don't know him," I said. "Don't know anyone named Hackett, Brackett, Sackett, or whoever. For that matter I don't know nobody else named Tackett.

"Look, if you two want to work I'd like to hire you but I owe it to you to tell that we got troubles on the R Bar R. Rustlers. Ain't nobody been killed yet but we've lost cows and a couple of hands quit after someone took a shot at 'em. I just hired on a couple of days ago. Ranch has a lady boss, but she's good folks. I told her I'd help her out and find some hands that wasn't afeered to fight."

The two looked at each other. "We don't pretend to be gunfighters," Lew Haight said. "But we don't mind a fight and when we hire on we ride for the brand. We don't scare too easy, neither."

"Good enough," I said. "Wages are thirty a month and found. Now I got me another job to do. You boys pick up your things and I'll meet you back here in about an hour and then we'll head for the ranch."

I downed the last of my beer, went out and climbed on Old Dobbin, and headed up the street to Nora's place. I tied Old Dobbin in the shade of a big cottonwood, went up the steps, opened the door and went in. The door opened into the front parlor and Nora herself was there to greet me. She was a statuesque woman of about fifty but she'd held her figure and her looks mighty well in the ten years or so she'd been there. Her hair was a coppery red, but I wouldn't have bet she was born that way. You could tell from looking at her she didn't get out in the sun much so she didn't have any of those sun wrinkles so many dry country women get.

The parlor was a big room and comfortable, with soft chairs and a pair of divans and several oil paintings on the walls, mostly of pretty women, lying back kind of relaxed and without much on in the way of clothes. Ma wouldn't have approved of me being in a place like that.

Nora recognized me right off. "Howdy, cowboy," she said. "You here for pleasure or to ask Mary Lou to do your laundry?"

I grinned at her. "Neither one," I said. "I come to ask a favor."

"Favors here usually cost money," Nora said, smiling a little.

"I wanted to talk to you about Mary Lou."

"She's busy right now. One of the R Bar R boys."

I started to say that none of our riders were in town but then it hit me. Mary Lou was up there with Evan Stevens. I started to say I'd wait but just then I heard a woman's muffled cry and then a man cursing. Nora headed for the stairs and I was right behind her.

She charged into the first room off the stairs with me still right behind. Mary Lou was kind of huddled in one corner of the small room, one hand holding her face where she'd been hit and the other hand clutching a flimsy kimono around her. As we went in Stevens swung around. He was wearing less than Mary Lou but he seemed not to notice.

He had a snarl on his face and when he seen me he spat out, "You. What the hell do you want? Get out of here before I throw you out."

Me, I didn't want any trouble. I had business to tend to so I snaked my gun out of its holster and kind of lazy-like waved it at him.

"Tell you what," I said. "You get dressed and you get out of here."

He started to take a step toward me, but I steadied the gun with it pointed right at him. "Don't," I said.

He glared at me, but he wasn't no fool so he turned and began getting dressed. When he'd finished I waved him through the door and on his way. He turned at the bottom of the stairs.

"That's twice," he said. "There won't be a number three."

Nobody said anything until after Stevens left. Then Nora asked the girl what happened.

"He told me to do some things I didn't want to do," she said softly, not looking at either of us. "When I wouldn't, he hit me. With his fist."

She touched the side of her face gently. It was swollen and already beginning to change color.

"Get dressed and come downstairs and have a cup of tea. You'll feel better," Nora said.

We both went back downstairs.

"Sit down," she invited. "Would you like something to drink?"

"Just coffee," I said.

Nora picked up a silver bell from the table beside her chair and shook it. In answer to its ding-a-ling a Mexican woman appeared.

"Bring Mr. Tackett some coffee and bring in a pot of tea and two cups," she ordered.

The Mexican woman disappeared and Nora turned to me. "I suppose I should thank you," she said. "But I'm not certain you did me a favor. It's not good business to run my clients out of here at gunpoint."

I shrugged. "Sorry, ma'am. I just don't like to see a lady mistreated."

Nora laughed cynically. "This is no business for ladies," she said. "And I don't think it's any business for Mary Lou. She came here from Kansas City to live with an uncle, but when she arrived here he was dead. He didn't leave her anything. No Money. Nothing. There wasn't any work for a nice girl and, well, even a nice girl has to eat. She's only been here a few weeks."

"What I come for today was to talk to you about Mary Lou," I said. "Meaning no offense, the other day when she washed my clothes she didn't seem like the kind of girl you usually find in a place like this. And I had a job in mind I'd like to talk to her about if you didn't have no objections."

Just then we heard Mary Lou coming down the steps. Nora called her over and told her to sit down. At the same time the Mexican woman came in with a big silver tray which she set down on the table beside Nora's chair. Nora handed me a cup and saucer that appeared to me to be real china. The cup was filled with steaming hot coffee. I took a sip. It was strong as a ox and it tasted good. Nora poured tea for herself and Mary Lou and after taking a sip told the girl, "Mr. Tackett wants to talk to you."

Mary Lou looked at me inquiringly. By now the bruise on the side of her face was turning purple, but I noticed even more the sad look in her blue eyes.

"Mary Lou," I said. "Can you cook?"

"I'm a good cook," she said.

"Can you sew and keep house?"

Before she could answer, Nora laughed, this time with real amusement. "If you're proposing marriage that's a funny way to go about it," she said.

My face turned warm and I knowed I was blushing. "No ma'am," I said. "I'm fixin' to ask her if she'd like a job, but I got to know first if she can do the things that need to be done."

I turned back to Mary Lou. "I'm ramroddin'" the R Bar R up the road a piece. It's run by a good lady not much older than you. But she's all alone out there, which ain't good. A woman ought not to be alone that far from town. I was wonderin' if you'd like to come out there and help around the place. Do the cookin' and help with the housework and keep Miss Esme company. Pay you the same as a puncher, thirty dollars a month and found. Course I'd have to clear it with Miss Esme first."

She looked at me disbelievingly, then a tear appeared at the corner of one eye.

"Would she have me?" she asked, her voice quavering. "I'm

nothing but a—but a—." She stopped and covered her face with her hands and I saw her shoulders shaking.

"I think so," I said. "Miss Esme's a good lady. And she needs help and company. No woman should have to live alone like that. I'll talk to her tonight and if she says she wants you I'll send Billy Bob in with the wagon tomorrow."

I thanked Nora, picked up my beat-up old hat, and headed for the door. As I went out Nora called after me, "Come back sometime when you can stay awhile."

I climbed on Old Dobbin and we headed back to the Rocking Horse saloon where I found Lew Haight and Blackie Harrington waiting. They were saddled up and ready to go.

We took off north toward the R Bar R, but we'd gone less than a mile when I suddenly swung east and away from the trail about half a mile. There was sagebrush and several kinds of cactus scattered about but it was easy riding for the most part. I pulled up for a minute while I rolled a cigarette and explained. "I've had run-ins with a couple of tough hombres in the last few days. Wouldn't put it past neither of them to think about bushwhackin' a man. If either one of 'em's thinkin' that way this'll make it a little harder for him."

I figured if one of them was out there it would be Stevens. He was one of those dangerous men I wouldn't put nothing past. Besides, Jack Sears was nursing a broken hand and that meant he wouldn't be using a rifle for a while.

Four hours later when we rode into the R Bar R we hadn't seen a soul. Billy Bob was standing outside the bunkhouse when we rode in and I noticed he was wearing two guns, the one on his left side had its butt forward for a cross draw. Billy Bob wasn't as young as he used to be and he only had one arm, but you could see he wasn't a man to take lightly in time of trouble.

I introduced him to Lew and Blackie and showed them where to stow their gear whilst Billy Bob hurried up to the house to tell Esme there would be two extra hands for supper. By the time we'd unsaddled and turned the horses into the corral it was time to wash up. When we finished that I taken the boys into the kitchen to meet Esme. She was just finishing putting dinner on the table and her face lighted up when she saw Lew and Blackie.

"I was lucky," I told her. "Lew and Blackie was just waitin' around to be hired. They ain't afeered of a fight, either."

"Oh," she said. "I hope there won't be any fighting. Maybe now that you boys are here the rustlers will go away."

"I wouldn't count on it," Billy Bob said grimly. "Of all the ranches in this part of the country we look like the easiest pickings."

I suddenly realized that I didn't know hardly anything about the country and the ranches around Nora. I'd drifted into the country less than a week ago and hadn't planned on staying. In fact I hadn't planned on much of anything. I still had a few dollars in my jeans from the job I'd had up in Lodestone and I was just riding free, wanting to see some more of the country before I needed to go to work again. I hadn't been looking for the job at the R Bar R and if we could get some good hands and chase out the rustlers, well, I'd be moving on again.

But as long as I'd taken the job I figured I'd better get to know the lay of the land. So we spent the rest of dinner talking about the country around Nora, what other ranches there were, and who owned them. This was dry country although the Little Colorado starting from the south of us flowed north and west until it joined the Colorado, and there was a few streams came out of the mountains along the continental divide. In a wet year some of them even flowed all summer.

Colonel Rankin had an on-and-off stream running several miles through the land he ran cattle on. He'd dammed some washes here and there to hold the water and at the ranch he'd dug the well for the house and another one for the stock and for whatever else it might be needed for. It was good water, too, cold and sweet.

I had noticed a few cattle from time to time on the way back from Nora but hadn't got close enough to see any brands, and once, off in the distance, I thought I saw some ranch buildings.

Turned out there was three other ranches north of Nora. None of them had the water the R Bar R had and only one, the Lazy A, was a real going concern.

It was owned by a man named Fink who'd come into the country with a couple thousand head of cattle about three years back. He bought out the previous owner of the Lazy A and had gone to work fixing up the ranch and building his herd. The way Esme told it he was a solid sort, about thirty-five and single. He'd been by the R bar R a few times but hadn't really come courting. Esme sounded a little disappointed when she said that. I couldn't really blame her. It was a lonesome land and she was a lone and lonesome woman.

The other two ranches, the Bar BQ and the AMA, were ramshackle, rawhide outfits, running a few cattle up against the mountains south and east of the R Bar R and just barely hanging on. Sounded to me like we ought to take a look see for some R Bar R cattle that might have drifted over their way, likely with some help. Tomorrow, me and the boys would start looking around and begin pushing R Bar R steers back toward the middle of our range.

We chewed the fat a while after supper and then I told the boys I needed to talk to Miss Esme, and they headed out to the bunk-house.

When they were gone I came right to the point. I told Esme I didn't like the idea of her being here all alone most days, nor did I think it right that she had to run the ranch and do the cook-ing, too.

"Is there something wrong with my cooking?" she asked inno-cently.

"No ma'am," I said. "It's as good cookin' as I ever et, but you oughtn't to be cookin' for the hired hands and keepin' this house and trying to run the ranch and keep the books and all, too."

"What do you suggest?" she asked.

"I want to bring a woman out here and pay her to help you," I said.

Then I plunged right in. "I've found one who'll come. She needs a job. Says she can cook and keep house and anything else that needs doing. She's about your age. Not real purty, but she's neat and she talks good. There's only one thing . . ."

I hesitated.

"Yes?" Esme said with that question in her voice.

"I don't rightly know how to say it," I said. "She come to town a few weeks ago but the kinfolk she thought she had here was gone. And, well, she didn't have no money and no job and, well . . ." I stumbled around and hemmed and hawed a bit, then I spit it out. "She went to work at Nora's."

She didn't speak for a minute. Then she said, "And you want to bring her out here?"

"Yes'm," I said. "Look. She's just a kid. She was broke and desperate. You know how it is."

"No," she said. "I don't."

"You won't take her on?"

"No," she said. "I'm disappointed that you would ask me to. She's a—."

"Don't say it," I said. "I know what she is. So does she. And she ain't proud of it. But, well, when you get hungry enough . . ."

I left it hanging right there, stood up and turned to go.

"Wait," she said suddenly. "You're right, Del. I've never gone hungry, never worried about my next meal or my next dollar. I don't know how it is. I don't know what I'd do if it came to that. I'll give her a try and see if she works out. But if she doesn't or if she gets to doing uh, well, you know what with the boys, then she goes.

"But you're right, I do need help and I could certainly use some company. It gets pretty lonely out here."

She paused a second and then added: I'll expect two things from her. That she act like a lady and that she earn her keep."

"I'll send Billy Bob in with the wagon tomorrow to bring her out," I said.

CHAPTER 3

NEXT MORNING after breakfast I taken Billy Bob aside and told him the situation.

"I want you to take the wagon into town and get that girl and her things out here as quick as you can. And I don't want no talk about where she come from or what she's been doin', either from you or her. We'll know soon enough if either Lew or Blackie has seen her at Nora's. If they have then there's one or two more who're going to have to keep their mouths shut.

"And, by the way, find out her last name. I never thought to ask."

After he'd left I went back up to the house and knocked on the front door. Esme opened it and I went in to the big living room. It was a man's room with heavy leather chairs and oak tables and such, some of which looked handmade. There was a big solid oak rolltop desk over in one corner and it was clear that Esme had been doing some book work. There was also a huge fireplace.

"You up to goin' for a ride?" I asked her. "I want to take a look at your range and there may be some things you can show me."

"I'll change my clothes and be ready in just a few minutes," she said, and then asked, "Is Mary Lou coming today?"

I told her I'd sent Billy Bob to pick her up. I went back outside and while I was waiting for her to get ready I gave Lew and Blackie their orders.

"Stick close to the house today," I said. "Til we get a better feel about the rustlers I don't want to leave this place unguarded.

"Another thing, a feller named Evan Stevens quit here in a huff yesterday and then him and me had a little run-in in town. He's a mean bad man and I don't want him comin' back here with any ideas about botherin' Miss Esme or doin' somethin' to the ranch. Instead of loafin' you can chop some kindling for the cook stove and look around and see what needs fixin' and cleanin' up.

"I hired a girl in town yesterday to come out here and work for Miss Esme and keep her company. It ain't good for a woman to be alone out here in the middle of nowhere. Billy Bob's gone to town to get her. Name is Mary Lou. She's young and not exactly ugly and you two are to keep your hands offn her."

They both gave me a funny look. "And that goes for me, too," I added, and they both laughed.

About then Esme came out, wearing blue jeans that looked like something that feller in San Francisco—Levi somebody or other—was making for miners and cowboys and such, with cute little copper rivets at the corners of the pockets. Tucked into her jeans was a man's checked shirt that was too big for her but didn't entirely hide what she had, and she wore high heeled boots. Purty as a picture. She was carrying a sack that looked like it had food in it. I hoped so. I can go without if I have to, but I'm not a man who enjoys going hungry.

She kept her horse in the barn, an Appaloosa gelding she called Baby, and I'd saddled him while the boys and me were talking.

As she came up I said, "If you got a rifle, be a good idea if you brought it along. Can't tell what kind of varmints we might run into."

She turned and hurried back to the house. I watched her as she went. It occurred to me she looked as good from the back as she did from the front. I shook my head in annoyance and reminded myself that she owned the ranch and even if I was the honcho I still wasn't nothing but a hired hand.

She came back in a minute with a Winchester that looked like it had been used a time or two, shoved it into a boot alongside the saddle, and swung aboard without any help from me. She was riding astride, man style, and she led off, swinging wide and around behind the ranch house toward the mountains. This was high country, anyway, but the mountains loomed up considerably higher, maybe five or six thousand feet. There was still snow on their peaks. I wondered if it ever entirely melted.

This normally was dry country until you got right up against the mountains and here in late May on the flatland there wasn't much grass left, nor were there many cattle. The horses weaved their way through the sagebrush and the occasional pear and barrel cactus that dotted the range. We climbed gradually but steadily for an hour and by the end of that time there was a scattering of cattle including a number of calves that were still following their mothers around. Up here the grass was more plentiful and the country was beginning to get more rugged. Ahead of us there were three canyons heading back into the mountain, their sides dotted with pine and fir that seemed to get thicker the higher the canyons went.

I asked Esme how far back the canyons went and if she knew what was back there. Turned out she hadn't taken the time to go exploring. She'd been going to school in Virginia, which was where the colonel had been born, until a year ago, when she'd come West to be with her father. She'd only been here a couple of months when all the trouble started. First, cattle had begun disappearing, then the horse had dragged her pa, then the random shooting had begun, scaring off all her hands but Billy Bob Doyle and Evan Stevens.

Even though her father had been in the west for more than twenty years, both as a soldier and a rancher, she'd pretty much grown up in the east, going to school most of the year and spending summers with relatives down near Manassas.

"I don't know very much about ranching," she said. "I've been relying a lot on Billy Bob and Evan Stevens, but I never quite liked or trusted Evan even though Father seemed to. I didn't like the way he looked at me, and after Father was killed I didn't like the way he acted, almost as if he owned the ranch—and me."

She turned and looked at me. "I'm glad you came along," she said.

We'd stopped in the shade of a big old cottonwood that was growing along the edge of a wash. The day was beginning to get warm and I was reaching for my canteen when of a sudden for just a fraction of second I caught a tiny bit of sun reflecting off something up ahead maybe three hundred yards in a clump of scrub trees.

"Get off your horse," I said. "Act natural but get off your horse and get behind that tree. Now!"

She started to swing down and I touched my spurs to Old Dobbin and taken off at a gallop to where I'd spotted the reflection. Dobbin hadn't taken more than half a dozen jumps when I heard something buzz by my head that wasn't no bee and at the same time there was the crack of a rifle from up ahead. Whoever he was fired once more, then I heard the sound of hoofs and caught a glimpse of a roan horse and a rider in a tan shirt and he was headed lickety-split for that middle canyon which lay dead ahead of us.

I pulled up. Wasn't any sense in following him into that canyon where he could easy lay a trap for me. Besides Esme was back there by the cottonwood and it wouldn't be smart to leave her alone with a gang of gun-happy rustlers running around loose and pot-shooting at anyone they saw.

I trotted on up to where the bushwhacker had been waiting, swung down from Old Dobbin, and began a careful look around. It didn't take long to find where he'd been waiting. There was the butt of a cigarette on the ground and a burned-out farmer match near by. There was also bootprints, but they didn't show me much, average size and not sunk in much, like he was just average weight, too.

I found where he'd kneeled behind a rock which made a good resting place for his rifle and I found a couple of spent .30 caliber shells, also nothing out of the ordinary. I saw he had taken off running to his horse which was tethered nearby and it, in turn, had started off at a dead gallop, like he'd really sunk his spurs to it. There was no way to tell if he was trying to shoot one of us or just scare us, but it was clear that he didn't want to stand and fight.

It puzzled me why he was waiting there. How come he knew we were going to be riding this way? For a minute I thought to backtrack him but Esme was back there alone and I didn't want her worrying. I climbed on Old Dobbin and cantered on back to where I'd left her. She was gone. Her horse was tied to a small bush but she was gone. Now what in tarnation had happened to that girl? I scratched my head in puzzlement and was just beginning to look around when I heard her voice coming from the direction of the wash.

"I'm glad it's you," she said, and I could hear the relief in her voice. "You were gone longer than I thought you'd be and I was afraid something had happened."

She tossed her rifle onto the bank and I leaned down and grabbed her hand and hauled her up beside me. She reached down and picked up the rifle. "I don't know if I could have used this on a man or not," she said. "I'm glad I didn't have to find out."

Coming back to her I'd had a chance to see how far we'd come, and it was maybe six miles, climbing all the time. We were at least a thousand feet higher than the ranch and in this air the buildings stood out sharp and clear. I turned and looked up at the head of Middleton Canyon which was the one we'd been aiming at. On the way Esme had named all three canyons for me. The one on the north, to my left, was Green Tree Canyon and the southern one, on my right was called Sweet Springs. Esme said her father had told her that about a mile up the canyon was spring of cold, sweet water and forty or fifty acres of good grazing where he bunched some of his cows in the summetime.

From where we stood the ground has begun to steepen all the way to the opening of Middleton Canyon and it was easy to see how a man with a pair of binoculars could keep a close eye on the ranch and any riders headed this way. That was one easy mystery solved. The other one—what was up in Middleton Canyon that we weren't supposed to see—would have to wait.

We turned and angled north toward the mouth of Green Tree canyon and by noon we were picking our way between the trees and rocks along the south side of the canyon. I pulled up in a little open space where there was good grazing for Old Dobbin and Baby. A trickle of water seeped out of the rock along the canyon wall and dripped into a clear pool at the base of the rock. I dipped my finger in and tasted it. It was sweet and cold and tasted good.

"This is a lovely place for a picnic," Esme said, dismounting.

She got down the sack I'd seen that morning and fished out a red-and-white checkered cloth which she spread on the grass. Then she got out some packages she'd wrapped in clean white flour sacking and opened them up. There was a couple of thick ham sandwiches and when we'd finished them—I ate half of Esme's—she opened the other one and out fell half a dozen doughnuts.

I hadn't had a doughnut since I'd left Lodestone and Ma twelve years ago. Ma hadn't been much of a cook but she baked a good apple pie and made the best doughnuts in the gold country and I'd often longed for a taste of them during my wanderings. I made a pig of myself on them doughnuts—ate five of them.

I saw Esme smiling at me as I was stuffing the remains of the last one into my mouth. I felt myself turning red.

"I guess I hogged those doughnuts, but they sure were good. First I've had since I left home."

"I'm glad you liked them," she said. "Father loved them. They're from an old family recipe I brought with me from Virginia."

She switched subjects then. "Where are you from, Del?" she asked. "When did you leave home?"

Suddenly, I felt like a fool. What was I doing out here with this pretty young woman, anyway? She was well-bred and well educated. I come out of the Sierra gold fields and didn't even know who my father was. I hadn't had no formal education. I could read just a bare little bit—printing mainly—and write my name if I wasn't in a hurry, and do a few sums, but not much more.

Most of my education had come the hard way, working in the gold fields, punching cows, riding shotgun, that sort of thing. I was good with a gun or a knife, good with my fists, and good with a rope. But that was about it. I sure didn't belong here with this high-class girl, no matter how friendly she seemed toward me.

"Time we was goin'," I said. "Billy Bob will be back with Mary Lou any time now and you'll want to show her around in the daytime."

She started to say something but changed her mind and began putting things back in the sack. She was silent all the way back to the ranch and I knew she was upset that I wouldn't talk about myself. I shrugged my shoulders. I owed it to Esme to get the ranch in shape and see what could be done about the rustlers. But after that I'd be hitting the trail again. Esme might be the woman for me but I sure wasn't the man for her.

Billy Bob and Mary Lou were already at the ranch when we arrived. He'd set her small traveling trunk on the veranda and she'd been waiting there for us to come in from the range. She was wearing a plain gray dress and her blond hair was in pigtails. She looked more like somebody's sister than what she'd been. Esme dismounted and walked over to Mary Lou who'd come down the steps to greet us. She looked uneasy and was twisting her handkerchief nervously. It was plain she didn't know what to expect. Neither did I.

Esme walked up to her and started to extend her hand, then of a sudden she took a step closer and gathered Mary Lou in her arms. Mary Lou put her arms around Esme like a little girl and began to shake and quiver all over. I could see she was crying great gulping sobs. And Esme was stroking her hair and saying things like "There, there," and "It's all right now," and "You're home now."

I turned away, embarassed like, and headed for the bunkhouse. I hadn't taken but a few steps when Esme called, "Mr. Tackett, will you please bring Mary Lou's trunk into the house."

I took it into the spare bedroom and set it down. They both said, "Thank you, Mr. Tackett," but Mary Lou sounded a lot friendlier than Esme. Well, if that's the way it was going to be, that's the way it was going to be. I hadn't hired out to socialize; I'd hired out to run a ranch and run off some rustlers. Soon as I got that done I'd be moving along.

I went and checked up on what Blackie and Lew were doing. They'd been busy, chopping enough kindling for a couple of weeks, replacing three rotted-out fence posts, oiling the pump handle on the well and the hinges on the barn door, the bunkhouse door, and every other door they could find, and cleaning out the barn. They were good workers. I told them to knock it off for the day, and hollered at Billy Bob, who was rubbing down the two horses he'd used to go to town, to join us.

Sitting around the table in the bunkhouse I asked Billy Bob to sketch out a map of the R Bar R and place it in relation to the other ranches around and to Nora. One thing I'd found in my wanderings, a map could give you the lay of the land better than anyone could explain it. I'd gotten a little feel of the area in the last few days but I needed to know it better and also quicker than I'd learn it on horseback. It wasn't going to hurt for Lew and Blackie to know it, too.

It turned out that Colonel Rankin had been smart enough to homestead the quarter section where the ranchhouse stood. The rest he owned by right of possession and there was a lot of the rest.

Off to the west the land gradually got drier and drier and it wasn't too long before it became desert. In back of the ranch, to the east, his land stretched about five miles up to the base of the mountains and then as far back into the canyons as a steer could wander. Off to the north there wasn't anything for miles and the big job was to keep the cattle from wandering too far. To the south, between the R Bar R and Nora, twenty miles to the south, were the three ranches Billy Bob had told me about. There were ranches to the south of Nora, also, Billy Bob said, as well as some back in the mountains to the south and east. But it was spread out country. A lot of room and not many folks.

Tomorrow, I told them, I wanted Blackie and Lew to swing wide out toward the desert pushing any cattle they found back toward the ranch.

"Any water holes out there?" I asked Billy Bob.

"Two, mebbe three," he replied. "Depending on the time of year."

Using a piece of charcoal from the wood stove Billy Bob had drawn a crude map on the surface of the table, showing the ranch in location to the mountains, Nora to the south and the Little Colorado River off to the south and west beyond the Painted Desert. Now he marked the spots where there might still be water from the winter rains or any more recent.

"If there's water out there you might want to stay out for three or four days, otherwise come on in in the evenings," I told them.

Then I turned to Billy Bob. "I'd like you to hang around the ranch for now. Be a good time to show the ladies how to use a gun. Saddle their own horses and anything else that might come in handy if they get caught here alone. Probably nuthin' gonna happen but you never know."

"What about you?" Lew asked.

I told them then about being shot at. "I'm curious about Middleton Canyon," I said. "I want to find out what's up there and why somebody's tryin' to scare us off.

"What do you know about that place, Billy Bob?"

"Not much," he said. "Didn't think there was much to know. Was up it about halfway several times looking for steers first year I was here, but ain't been up it since. There's good grazin' in the lower part of it. But about halfway up it narrows down and gets pretty choked with brush and boulders. Lot of fir and pine up there too, some manzanita, and cottonwoods in the bottom. Never saw no sign of cattle up that way so never tried to fight my way to the top. You'd have to walk most of the way. Oh, yeah, there's a stream up there, too. Not much of one and it goes underground afore it reaches the mouth of the canyon."

Just then one of the women began beating on the iron triangle by the kitchen door.

"Dinner bell," Billy Bob said. I headed for the wash basin to clean up a mite then joined the rest of them in the kitchen.

There'd been a change. Esme was sitting at the head of the table and Mary Lou was serving dinner. Except for the bruise on her cheek where Stevens had hit her she was a pretty girl, prettier than I remembered her. And she was working with a smile on her face. No doubt about it, she was glad to be here and away from Nora's. It was plain, too, that she hadn't run into Blackie or Lew whilst she was working for Nora.

After she put the food on the table Esme asked her to eat with the rest of us. When she'd sat down Esme introduced her as Mary Lou Schmidt and said she'd be living there and doing the cooking and helping with the work around the house. Then she added: "And I expect you to treat her the same way you treat me—as a lady and with respect."

Mary Lou turned red, all embarassed, but the boys nodded and dug in. If anything, Mary Lou was a better cook than Esme. When Lew commented on her cooking she explained she grown up on a farm in Illinois and she done the cooking for her Pa and the hired hands from the time she was thirteen when her ma had died.

Turned out her pa had died just a few months back, when she was 18, leaving the farm to his second wife who didn't want her around. She'd come to Nora, she said, to live with an uncle only to find that he, too, had died, leaving her without kinfolk or a place to live.

"You came along just in time," she said to Esme. "I'm so grateful."

That made me feel good. The R Bar R was beginning to get an outfit put together and it looked like Mary Lou was going to fit in real well. Now all I had to do was to find that rustler hideout and see what we were up against there. After I found them—well, I didn't have that figured out yet. Nearest law was at least fifty miles in any direction and I wasn't no big supporter of Judge Lynch. But first things first. Tomorrow I was going to take a look at Middleton Canyon. It would be easier without no woman around.

As far as Esme being angry with me went, I hoped she'd get over it. Regardless, I wasn't comfortable talking about me and Ma and where we'd come from. I hadn't had no schooling and I didn't have no father and I was ashamed of both of them things. I'd work for her and help her and maybe kind of wish for her from a distance, but I wasn't never going to be part of her life and I knew it.

CHAPTER 4

As USUAL, I was up at the first sign of daylight and fifteen minutes later I was saddling Old Dobbin. As I led him out of the stable door I noticed a light in the kitchen window. Tying Old Dobbin to the hitching rail, I walked over to the kitchen door, knocked once, and went on in.

Mary Lou was dressed and all shiny-faced with her blond hair done up in those twin braids. She had a fire going in the stove and she'd just put a pot on for coffee.

"You're up early," she said.

"I was ridin' out and saw the light in the window and thought maybe I could get a cup of coffee afore I went."

"Mr. Tackett," she said, "I'm most grateful to you for what you did. I'll never be able to make it up to you, but I'm going to try."

I was touched. "You're doin' real good, Mary Lou," I said. "You hang in here and do a good job helpin' Miss Esme and afore long what you been through won't be nothin' but a bad dream."

She started to move toward me like she wanted me to take her in my arms and comfort her, which I wasn't anxious to do, what with Esme due to walk through the door at any minute, or so I thought.

"Coffee smells like it's about ready," I said, grabbing a chair and quick sitting down. She turned away, took a big, heavy mug, filled it to the brim, and set it in front of me. I picked it up and sipped it. It tasted good.

"Could I fix you something to eat before you go?" she asked.

"You might put me together a samwich I could carry along," I said. "A body can get mighty hungry after he's been ridin' half a day."

Just then Esme came through the door. "Oh," she said. "I hope I'm not interrupting anything."

"Nope," I said. "I just stopped in for a cup of coffee afore I head up to Middleton Canyon and Mary Lou offered to fix me a bait of food to take along, so I'm waitin'. Ain't much for goin' hungry less'n I have to."

It struck me again that she was sure a good-looking woman with a figure that wouldn't quit, and I had a hard time taking my eyes off her. I could understand Evan Stevens wishing there'd come a time when she'd be his. I concentrated on drinking my coffee until Mary Lou had made and wrapped a couple of beef sandwiches and had set them in front of me.

"Thanks, Mary Lou," I said. "That's mighty kind of you."

I stood up and turned to Esme. "I'll be shovin' off. If I don't come home tonight don't worry none. It may be I have to be gone two or three days. Blackie and Lew'll be out on the dry side movin' cattle toward the hills and Billy Bob'll be workin' around the place here. I've asked him to take some time and show the both of you somethin' about handlin' a rifle and a pistol."

I reached for my hat which I'd hung on a peg by the kitchen door and started out. Esme followed me out. She kind of tugged at my sleeve, so I stopped and turned, waiting for her to say something. She came right to the point, which, I'd noticed, was a habit of hers.

"What are you hiding, Del?" she asked. "Why don't you want to tell me about yourself?"

I felt myself beginning to get mad. But I taken hold of my temper and said evenly:

"Miss Esme, I got nothin' to hide. I ain't wanted by the law. I haven't done nothin' wrong. I've killed a few men. I didn't like it, but I didn't have no choice. I been workin' on my own since I was sixteen, punchin' cows, drivin' a stage and ridin' shotgun, doing a little bit of mining. I've fit a few Injuns and I was a deputy sheriff once for about a year. Where I come from—beggin' your pardon—ain't nobody's business. Where I'm going the good Lord only knows, but one day after we've got this ranch in shape I'll be drifting along, just like them tumbleweeds out there. Right now I've got work to do and I best be gettin' to it."

I unhitched Old Dobbin, tossed the reins over his head and climbed into the saddle.

"So long," I said and touched him lightly with my spurs.

Old Dobbin wanted to run so I taken off at a gallop, heading around in back of the ranch. After a few minutes I slowed him down to a fast, mile-eating trot and by the time the sun was coming up from behind the mountains I'd reached the spot where Esme and I had stopped under the shade of the old cottonwood tree. I drew up and studied the land ahead. The canyons were still in deep shadow. I eyed them while I pondered a minute how best to approach Middleton Canyon without someone taking a shot at me.

Then I headed for Green Tree Canyon, the same one where Esme and I had picnicked yesterday. Two hundred yards up from the spot where we'd eaten the canyon narrowed and steepened and the rocks and trees were too close together for even a mule to pick his way. Dismounting behind a huge rock that hid Old Dobbin from the view of anyone riding up the canyon, I tied him loosely to a tree, figuring if I never came back he'd eventually pull free and head for home.

Then I reached into a saddlebag, fishing for a pair of moccasins I kept there. While exploring for them my fingers hit that old diary that Ma had left and I hadn't gotten around to looking at. I told myself I had to do it one day soon. Might tell me something about who I was and where I was from. Trouble was, I couldn't read handwriting hardly at all and Ma would have written in longhand which was going to be mighty hard for me to figure out. Now wasn't the time, anyway. I pushed it aside and took out my moccasins and put them on. I tied my boots together with a piggin string and hung them around the saddle horn.

Giving Old Dobbin a last pat, I turned and headed up the canyon. It was slow going, making my way between and around the rocks and trees. I was carrying my rifle which also slowed me down and I was keeping a careful lookout for rattlers which would be plentiful in this country this time of year. If one bit me I wouldn't have much chance of coming out of there alive.

I'd gone about a mile up the canyon when it suddenly steepened even more and for a hundred yards or so I had to use handholds on trees and rocks to pull myself. Suddenly I broke through the trees and found myself looking down into a hanging valley that seemed to be about half a mile wide and stretched for at least two miles off to the south. It was lush with mountain grass and wildflowers and everywhere I looked there were white-faced cattle grazing. Nowhere did I see any riders, which wasn't surprising. Wasn't no reason for those cows to be going anywhere anyways.

I hadn't seen a hint of the valley from down on the flatland or coming up the canyon. The irregular lip on its lower side, rimmed with trees as it was, blended perfectly with the forest on the mountainside above it.

After a quick look I faded back down below the rim and hunkered down with my back to a tree whilst I studied on the situation.

One thing was plain, whoever was rustling R Bar R cattle had found a near-perfect holding place for them. Trouble was, unless there was an outlet at the south end of the valley or someone had found a pass from the valley over the mountains into New Mexico there wasn't any way to get those cows to market except through R Bar R land.

I knew now what I was going to have to do. I was going to have to locate the entrance to the valley that I assumed was at the upper end of Middleton Canyon. Then I was going to have to see if there was any other way to get in and out of the valley. And third, I was going to have to find out if the rustlers kept someone up here all the time and if they did where did he or they hole up.

Even that wasn't all. Before I was through I was going to have to find out who was behind the rustling. Do no good to get the cattle back if whoever was stealing them started stealing them all over again.

From where I was I started moving north, figuring to come to the north end of the valley, head up the mountain, and then make my way south along the upper rim. I figured that way I could spot any hideout the rustlers might have as well as the opening into the valley from below without stumbling by accident onto anyone guarding the opening.

It was the long way and it meant I probably wouldn't get back to the ranch tonight, but it wouldn't be the first night I'd slept out with only the sky and maybe some cut branches for a blanket. I'd left the sandwiches Mary Lou had made in my saddlebags and they were hanging on my saddle which was cinched firmly on top of Old Dobbin. He was less than a mile away as the crow flies, but I never was no crow. Looked like I'd be going hungry a while unless I came across a sandwich tree, none of which, as far as I knew, grew around here.

I wasn't worried much about being seen unless I just happened to run across someone or some guard was looking at exactly the right spot at exactly the right time. Trees ringed that valley pretty much all the way around and I wasn't wearing anything that might reflect the sunlight. I picked up a handful of dirt and rubbed it over the barrel of my rifle just to make sure there wasn't no shine there.

Nevertheless, I moved with care, stopping every now and then to listen and to scan those parts of the valley I could see through the trees. The north end of the valley was farther than I thought it was and at the end of it it kind of curved around the mountain on the north side. Then it surprised me by sloping gradually into a canyon I hadn't known was there that ran down the mountain in a north-south direction.

Suddenly, I saw them, three shiny lines running low through the trees that stood in the area between the high end of the canyon and the northeast end of the valley. I thought I knew what they were even though I'd never seen any before. I edged down to where I could get a good look. Sure enough, it was barbed wire. I'd heard they were beginning to use it down in Texas and southern New Mexico where there had been some real range wars in places like Lincoln County and down around the Apple Canyon country next to the Texas-Mexico border, but nobody I knew of was using it up this way yet, even though I knew it was sure to come.

The rustlers had strung three strands of it across the opening into the canyon to keep the cattle in the valley. But I noticed there were cattle hoofprints on the outside of the wire heading down the canyon. Here was the way, at least one of the ways, they were taking the stolen cattle out of the valley. I had no idea where they were being driven and today wasn't the day to find out. I wanted to make a circle of the valley first. Then, after I got back to the ranch tomorrow I would sit down with Billy Bob and see if he knew what lay to the north and east behind the mountain—Early Mountain, Billy Bob had said it was called.

Trouble is, I didn't get back to the ranch.

The sight of that barbed wire made me careless. Without warning something smashed me a wicked blow alongside of my head and, as though it were far away, I heard the sound of a shot. Next thing I knew I was sprawled on the ground, face down, my mouth half full of dirt and leaves. I couldn't move. I was paralyzed.

Then I heard voices coming closer. One said, "Better be careful. Might be a good idea to plug him again."

The second one said, "Naw. I got him dead to rights. Right through the head. No sense in wastin' a bullet."

Voice One said, "Who do you reckon he was, snoopin' around here like that?"

I felt the toe of a boot push roughly under me and then try to lift me up and turn me over. He got me just far enough to see the side of my face before he gave up and pulled his foot away.

There was the shock of recognition in the voice of Number One.

"It's that feller who beat up that tinhorn gunman, Jack Sears, down in Nora a while back. Name is Hackett or Sackett or something like that. I heered he hooked on with the R Bar R. It's a good thing you nailed him."

The second voice asked, "What do you think we ought to do with him? Ain't got no shovel. Ain't in the mood to dig, noways."

Voice One said, "Leave him there for the buzzards and coyotes and other varmints. Take his guns and let's get on back to the cabin. Evan ought to be comin' along pretty soon. He should of been here yesterday. He kin tell us about this feller, whether he's ridin' for the R Bar."

Voice Two said, "Time he was marryin' that uppity Rankin gal and puttin' an end to this nonsense. Boss says he should have had her hog-tied and branded by now. Funny the boss doesn't make a play for her hisself. Goodlookin' feller like him."

One of them shoved me roughly to get at my six-gun, yanked it out of the holster, and said, "Let's get out of here."

Their voices faded in the distance and I just kind of faded out.

I don't know how long I was unconscious, but when I came to the trees were throwing long shadows and it was noticeably cooler. My head was one big squeeze box, going in and out, not producing any music but throwing off more pain than I could remember.

For a minute I didn't know where I was, but then it gradually came to me. I'd been shot. There'd been two of them and they thought they'd killed me. And they'd taken my gun. I tried to move my right arm and it moved. So did the left one. A flood of relief flowed through me. I wasn't paralyzed. I reached up and gingerly felt the right side of my head. It was caked with blood. Whoever had shot me had missed by less than an inch blowing my brains out. As it was I'd have a permanent scar there both wide and deep. Well, it was better than being dead.

At that minute I wasn't worrying about a scar. I had plenty of them including that knife scar on my left cheek. I was worried about staying alive. Whoever it was who shot me might have a change of heart and come back with a shovel after all.

I put my arms under me and tried to push myself up. My head felt like two hammers were pounding on it, one from the inside and the other on the outside. I finally managed to struggle to a sitting position and looked around to see where I was. My eyes wouldn't focus and it was clear that bullet had not only torn my scalp open it had also left me with a concussion.

I sat there trying to figure out what to do and I was scared. Not only were my eyes blurry but I still hadn't cleared the cobwebs from my brain. But I knew one thing—I had to get out of there.

I inched my way to the nearest tree and holding on to its trunk I managed to pull myself to my feet. I was beginning to see things clearer now, and was remembering better where I was and how I'd gotten there. I figured the thing I'd better do was see if I could get back to Old Dobbin before he got tired of waiting for me and pulled loose and headed for home.

I hadn't taken more than two or three steps before I was overcome by dizziness. I grabbed at the nearest tree and hung on until my head cleared, but as soon as I tried taking another step the dizziness hit me again. I knew then I wasn't going to make it unless I could find a place close by to lie up for a few hours and let my head clear. I looked around and off to one side I saw where a huge fir tree had fallen bringing some smaller trees down with it, creating a tangled jungle of dead branches.

I started toward it, tottering from tree to tree and holding on to each one until I could shake off my dizzy spell. There at the end, with just a few feet to go, I sank down on my hands and knees and crawled the rest of the way. I managed to crawl to the far side of that big, dead trunk and there I found a little hollow half covered by the trunk and filled with dead and rotting leaves from last fall and several falls before. I crawled into it, pulling a few dead branches in behind me, and fell into a dead sleep.

Raindrops filtering through the branches finally woke me. It was dark and there was thunder rumbling between great flashes of lightning and of a sudden the rain was coming down in heavy sheets. It was one of those quick mountain storms and after about fifteen minutes the thunder moved away in the distance and it wasn't long after that the rain stopped. By this time I was soaked through and feeling miserable. But the rain had been heavy enough so that it cooled my face which was burning with fever and I even managed to catch some in my mouth and hands.

It was pitch black and I was disoriented. I wasn't sure what direction I'd taken when I staggered away from the place I'd been shot. All I'd known at the time was that I had to get away. I burrowed deeper into the leaves and snuggled closer against the tree trunk. After a bit I dropped off to sleep again. When I awoke it was full daylight. I was cold and hungry and thirsty. My head throbbed and I was kicking myself that I'd ever met up with Billy Bob and Esme and the rest of the people back at the R Bar R who were snug and warm and well fed.

One thing, the pain in my head had settled down to a dull, steady ache. I was still feverish, though, my throat was parched and my lips were dry and cracked. First thing I needed was water. Then I had to get back down to Old Dobbin. I was in danger as long as I was up here.

I started to move when suddenly I heard a horse whinny.

Then I heard a voice, one I hadn't heard before, say loudly and angrily, "All right, if you killed him where in the hell is the body?"

He didn't sound more than forty or fifty feet away and I realized that I hadn't been able to get very far last night before I gave out.

I gave silent thanks for last night's hard rain which should have pretty well washed out my tracks. But, still, they were only a few feet away and I wasn't very hopeful that they wouldn't find me if they looked.

A second voice muttered something I didn't catch and the angry man spoke again. "If that was Tackett then you better damn well find him and kill him this time. He gets back to the R Bar R he could ruin everything I've planned. I'm headin' for Nora now. Got a buyer comin' in who I hear ain't too fussy and he'll take some of what we got up here off of my hands if we can drive 'em to the railroad."

That did it. There had to be a southern exit to this valley because the nearest railroad was down by Chambers, about seventy miles to the south. There was no way anyone could drive cattle down on the flat from the north end of the valley and head them south to Chambers without crossing the R Bar R. Chambers, I'd heard, was also where the nearest law was.

The angry man apparently taken off then, because I heard hoofbeats fade away to the north.

Then one of yesterday's voices said, "I ain't never seen Fink so mad. You and me got two choices. We can find Tackett and kill him or we can hightail it out of this country before Fink kills us."

The other one said, "I ain't afeered of Fink. I ain't seen no graveyards he's filled."

"You ain't looked in the right places. I've seen him in action and I ain't never seen anyone faster. Not never."

The other one spoke again. "You look around and if he ain't here see if you can pick up his tracks. He's probably trying to get out of here and head for the R Bar. I'm gonna see if he crawled through the bob wire and headed out that way. If you can't find him see if you can find his horse. He's gotta have one around here somewhere. If we get his horse we got him trapped. Hell, he ain't even armed."

He was only part right. They'd taken my gun all right but they hadn't seen no reason to search me and I still had my hideout knife strapped to my leg.

I reached down and eased that six-inch blade out of its scabbard. If one of them found me and came close enough I wasn't going to go without a fight.

I heard the man who'd stayed behind begin to thrash around in the brush. He was pretty cocky and wasn't trying to be quiet, knowing I was bad hurt and didn't have a gun.

Moving so as to make no noise I hitched around to lie on my left side with my knife in my right hand, hidden beneath a layer of leaves. I was lying with the wounded, bloody side of my head up just enough so I could sneak a peak if he came close. If he got close enough I was going to cut him if I got any kind of chance. Like I say, I don't like killing people or cutting on them, but he was looking to kill me and, like some other times in some other places, I didn't see as how I had much choice.

I heard him come around my side of the tree trunk. Then there was no movement. He must have stopped to see if there was any sign of me. Suddenly he spoke.

"By God, there you are. Don't look like you got very far afterall. I knew I'd gotten you."

I lay still, not moving a muscle, hardly breathing. I heard him tearing out the branches I'd pulled in behind me. Then I heard branches brush against his pant leg as he moved toward me. And then I could see his boots as he stood over me and his legs begin to move as he went to squat down for a closer look.

I wasn't going to have any better chance. No sooner had he squatted and bent over me than I whipped my right arm around, across his back and down. I felt the knife go in deep. He grunted in pain and surprise. Before he could move I twisted the knife and pulled it out and struck again, this time up a little higher and on his left side. It hit bone, then slid off and went between his ribs. He fell over me, his head hitting the tree trunk as he fell. I felt him twitch a bit, then lie still, sprawled across my side and back.

He was a big man and it took me a couple of minutes to crawl out from under him, me being weak from loss of blood and the effects of my wound. I was lucky he hadn't had a chance to shout out because sound carried a long way in that clear mountain air and his friend could have heard and come back shooting.

I was weak and dizzy by the time I had pulled free. But after a minute the earth settled down and I went to work stripping him of his gun and going through his pockets. But there wasn't anything in them to tell me who he was. Only things he had of any value were his gun and a fifty-cent piece which I put in my pocket. It didn't make any difference to him whether I took it or left it since I'd already taken the most valuable thing he had, his life.

I looked around and spotted his horse about fifty feet away, tied to a bush. I managed to walk to him without falling. He shied a bit when I got near, not from my looks, the man I'd killed wasn't no raving beauty, but from the smell of the blood. I spoke softly to him and eased up to him, patting his head and rubbing him behind his ears. When he'd settled down I untied his reins and holding tight to the saddle horn struggled aboard.

He had a half full canteen tied to his saddle and I taken a big swallow from it and then walked that spotted gelding out of there. I'd figured by now that there'd only been two rustlers stationed in the valley. One was looking for me outside the barbed wire and I'd killed the other. The third man, Fink, had taken off for his ranch so I figured my best bet was to head down the valley and find the high end of Middleton Canyon. From there it shouldn't be much trouble getting back to the ranch.

Even though I was pretty sure there weren't any more rustlers in the valley I stuck to the western edge dodging in and out among the trees. No sense in taking chances. I'd only ridden about fifteen minutes before I came across a trail running east and west at a right angle to me. I turned west and it wasn't but a few minutes before the trail wound around a huge boulder and headed down, out of the hidden valley. Here it was, the exit from the valley into Middleton canyon.

Despite last night's rains you could see the trail was well used both by horses and by cattle. It wasn't wide and it was winding but, hemmed in as it was on both sides, it would be easy to drive cattle up here a few at a time. No wonder they didn't want anyone from the R Bar R nosing around.

I gave my horse its head and let him pick his way down the trail while I tried to think things through. Fink. I'd heard the name somewhere, I just couldn't place it at the moment. All I knew was that he was the leader of the rustlers and he had a ranch around here somewhere. It began to come back to me now, Evan Stevens worked for him, too. He'd sent Stevens to work at the R Bar R to cosy up to the old colonel and Esme, both. He could keep track of what was going on that way and maybe Stevens could even work it so he could marry Esme and bring the ranch under Fink's control.

Hunger was beginning to gnaw at me and I was beginning to feel dizzy again. I hadn't had anything to eat since early yesterday and I lost a sight of blood from that head wound. I hoped I could hold on until I reached the ranch. I slumped in the saddle and held onto the horn with both hands as the horse continued to pick his way down the trail.

The canyon was beginning to widen out a bit but it was choked with rocks of all sizes, some nearly as big as a house, trees and brush and deadfalls. The trail wound its way around and through until the horse stepped through a narrow crevasse between two huge boulders and there we were out in that meadow Billy Bob had told me was there. There was a spring bubbling out of the rocks on the south side of the canyon and cutting its way through the meadow which looked to be at least five acres. I looked around and saw maybe thirty cows and steers grazing and it was easy now to see how the rustlers worked. They'd drift cattle a few at a time into the canyon and at their leisure drive them up the trail and into the secret valley.

I rode over to the stream and let the horse drink his fill. Then I climbed carefully down from his back, holding onto the horn to keep from falling. I tied him to a small tree which bordered the stream. Using the tree's trunk for support I lowered myself to my knees and crawled the few feet to the stream. First I had me a long cold drink and that water tasted good. Then I began bathing my face and the side of my head, mainly trying to wash off the caked blood which had smeared the side of my face and my neck. The wound itself was caked solid and I didn't touch it.

I was feeling a little better now, but not good enough to stand up without help, so I crawled over to the tree and was just reaching for it when a cold voice said, "Don't move, Tackett, or you're a dead man."

I froze. I wasn't in any shape to do anything else, and that voice sounded like it meant business. Next thing I knew he kicked me in the ribs hard. I hollered from the combination of pain and surprise and fell flat on my face. He kicked me again but this time I managed to keep my mouth shut.

"All right. You can sit up," he said, "but keep yer hands where I can see 'em."

Hurting as I was I managed to turn over and struggle to a sitting position and get my first look at my captor.

It was Jack Sears. I thought I'd recognized that voice. He had a week's growth of beard and a coat of dirt that it had taken him about that long to accumulate. His right hand, the one I had stomped on, was cradled in a filthy bandana that he was using for a sling. But the six-gun in his left hand was pointed straight at my head and unwavering.

"Lift that gun out of its holster veree carefully," he ordered.

I did. And tossed it off to one side like he gestured for me to do.

"You're a dead man, Tackett," he said.

I just looked at him.

"Looks like someone almost beat me to you," he said.

"Rustlers," I said. "You must be one of them."

He shook his head. "I've watched 'em come and go a couple of times. Found me a nice little cave over on the other side of the canyon. Big enough for me and my horse. Looks like Injuns used to use it. Got some kind of funny picture writin' on the walls. But I ain't no rustler. Just waiting for my hand to heal."

"Trouble with you is you talk too much," I said, reaching down to scratch my leg.

If I could just get that knife in my hands I could even this up a mite. He'd kill me for sure, but maybe I could get some steel into him first.

"If your goin' to kill me go ahead and do it now and get it over with."

I could see him smile through his beard. "Knowed of you a long time, Tackett. Heard about that hideout knife of yours, too." he said. "Reach down now and take it out veree carefully and toss it over by yer gun."

Again, I did what he told me to do. I was just about a dead man now, and I knew it, but Jack Sears was a talker and as long as he talked I'd stay alive and as long as I was alive maybe, just maybe I could stay that way.

"Damn you," he snarled suddenly. "You sneak punched me back there in Nora and you broke my hand when you stomped on it. I been hidin' out waitin' for it to heal so's I could find you and gut shoot you."

He leveled his gun right where my navel would be if he could see it and I tensed for the shot. Being gut shot is about as bad a way to die as I know. You die slow and painful, hoping someone will come along and put you out of your misery. Even so I wasn't going to give him the satisfaction of hearing me beg. I looked him right in the eye.

"Shoot and be damned," I said.

Unexpectedly, I saw his trigger finger relax and he lowered the gun.

"I'm a lot of things, but I ain't no murderer," he said. "Get on your horse and git. I'll come after you when I get my hand to workin' right."

Then he did something strange. He picked up my gun and knife, took the bullets out of the gun, and tossed it and my knife near to where I could reach them.

"Take 'em," he said. "But don't try nuthin'. I want you alive until I kin kill you myself."

Deliberately, he turned his back on me and stomped off across the meadow. I sat there for a moment, not moving. My head was pounding again and my forehead was hot. Where he'd kicked me with those pointed boots he wore it felt like a couple of ribs were broken or at least cracked.

I was sore, I was hurting, I was feverish, I was hungry and more than anything I was dead tired. All I really wanted to do was stay right where I was and sleep the clock around.

But I couldn't do that and I knew it. Any minute Jack Sears could change his mind and come back to finish the job he'd chickened out on a few minutes earlier. I crawled over to my weapons and stuck the gun back in my holster and my knife in its scabbard alongside my leg. Then I crawled over to my horse, clutched at a stirrup and struggled to my feet. After resting a minute I grapped the saddle horn with both hands and slowly and awkwardly and painfully crawled into the saddle. I turned the horse toward the mouth of the canyon and gigged him gently in his flanks.

"Come on, boy," I whispered. "Let's go home."

CHAPTER 5

THAT SPOTTED HORSE walked down to the mouth of the canyon and then, instead of heading for the R Bar R, took off at a tangent that would take us about ten miles south. He was going to his home, not to mine. I pulled on the reins and he reluctantly headed in the right direction.

It was late afternoon and the sun was a big orange ball sinking low over the desert. I swayed in the saddle from weakness and weariness, just hoping and praying I could hang on for another couple of hours. My head pounded, my ribs ached and I felt myself drifting in and out of consciousness.

Once I heard someone singing "Brennan on the Moor," an old Irish folk song Ma used to sing from time to time. It was me. Another time I felt myself sliding sidewise out of the saddle. I caught myself just in time. I don't know how long I rode; it seemed like forever. Arousing myself from my stupor, I noticed it had gotten dark. There was a light ahead that I thought at first was a star. Then I knew it wasn't. It was a light shining through a window.

"Lord, let it be the ranch," I prayed aloud, and fell off my horse.

I don't know how long I was unconscious, but when I came to I thought someone was washing my face. I opened my eyes and there was this dark shape hovering over me and licking my cheek. It was Beauty. And the ranch couldn't be too far away. I struggled painfully to my feet, spotted the light I'd seen earlier, and headed for it. I taken one step and fell again. I lay there too weak to move. After a bit I crawled to my knees and looked around. Beauty was gone and that spotted horse had wandered off. I wasn't more than a quarter of a mile from the ranch but it might as well have been on the moon.

Faintly, in the distance, I heard a dog barking and then I passed out again. When I next opened my eyes the morning sun was shining through the window and I was lying in a bed between white sheets. I knew I was dreaming so I closed my eyes and went back to sleep.

The next time I opened them I was looking into a pair of soft brown eyes. It was Beauty. She'd climbed up on the bed and was lying there panting gently and looking at me. I'd always had a way with dogs but this, I decided, was too much. Those eyes should have belonged to a girl, not any girl, but Esme. I reached outside the covers and patted her. She licked my hand.

Just then Esme's voice from the doorway said, "Beauty, get off the bed." Beauty thumped her tail on the spread a time or two, but didn't move.

"Beauty, you beast, I said get off the bed," she repeated with amusement.

Beauty stood up, yawned and stretched, and jumped off the bed. She went over to a corner and lay down. Esme came on into the room.

"You're awake," she said, commenting on the obvious, the way a lot of people do. "How are you feeling?"

"I'm sorry about Beauty," I said. "I didn't ask her up. She was there when I woke up.

"I guess she saved my life."

"I think she might have," Esme said. "We might not have found you otherwise. And you were in pretty bad shape."

"How long have I been here?"

"Today's the third day."

"That's a long time. I left Old Dobbin up in the canyon."

"He broke loose and came on in two days ago. He's in the barn and your saddlebags are over in the corner."

I reached up and touched my head where I'd been shot. It was bandaged heavily. She saw the gesture.

"It's healing nicely."

I started to sit up, but quickly sank back down. It's not that I couldn't have made it but I suddenly realized I didn't have any clothes on. Esme noticed my embarassment and giggled.

"Your clothes are folded up on that chair," she said, pointing to the only chair in the room.

I looked around. I was obviously in her father's bedroom. The furniture was the same kind of heavy oak that I'd seen in the living room. There was a dresser with a lamp on it, a shelf with a few books, and some pegs along one wall where some men's clothes and a Stetson hat were hanging.

I kind of squirmed down farther under the covers in an unconscious effort to keep my nakedness hidden. "Who," I asked. "Who—?"

"Blackie and Lew brought you in. They undressed you and put you to bed."

"If you would leave now I'll get up and get dressed," I said with as much dignity as I could muster.

She went to the chair, picked up my shirt and brought it over. It had been washed hard enough to get most of the dirt and blood out of it.

"Put it on," she ordered. "You'll be more comfortable. And then we can talk. Mary Lou washed your clothes. You can thank her later. They were pretty dirty."

"I been rollin' around in the dirt a lot," I said.

"I'll be back in a moment," she said and left.

I had the shirt on and buttoned by the time she came back.

She was carrying a big mug of hot coffee. I taken it from her and took a sip. It burned my lips, but it tasted good.

"Mary Lou will be in in a moment with soup and toast," she said. "After you've eaten maybe you'd like to try getting up."

I nodded yes and just then Mary Lou came in with a tray on which she'd put a big bowl of soup and two big chunks of bread which she'd fry-toasted in a skillet. She looked mighty pretty with her hair done in those two strands of braids. The bruise on her face had disappeared and been replaced by a happy look. She set the tray on my lap.

"Thank you, Mary Lou," I said. "That's mighty nice of you. And thanks for washin' my clothes."

"They were pretty dirty," she said.

"I been rollin' around in the dirt a lot," I said.

"I'm so glad you're all right," she said. "I don't know what we'd have done . . ." She left the sentence unfinished and hurried out the door.

Esme took my clothes and set them on top of the dresser and pulled the big chair over by the bed.

"What happened, Del?" she asked, sitting down. "Did someone try to kill you?"

Between spoonfuls of the soup, which was filled with potatoes and chunks of beef and dried vegetables, and bites of toast, I told her from the beginning what had happened, leaving out only the bit about Jack Sears, which was my problem but not one of hers.

She was amazed when I told her about that hidden valley. She'd never heard of it and didn't think the old colonel knew about it either.

"We clean those rustlers out and it will make for great summer grazing," I said.

When I mentioned Fink she was shocked. "That can't be Reggie Fink," she said. "He seems like such a nice man."

"I don't place him," I said. "Name sounds familiar but I don't place him."

"He owns the ranch about ten miles south of here," Esme said. "He moved in before I came here, about two years ago. We don't see much of him, he keeps pretty much to himself, but he's been here a few times and he's always been pleasant and polite.

"He's about thirty-five-years-old and is almost as big as you are. He's good-looking, too. He has wavy brown hair and a nice smile. He has beautiful white teeth."

"Father liked him," she added, an undertone of amusement in her voice.

"How big is his ranch? What's his brand?" I asked short-like. I didn't like pretty boys, maybe because I wasn't one. And I didn't like her liking them, either. All of a sudden I realized I was jealous. And that was stupid. I reminded myself again that this well-bred, well-educated girl wasn't for me. Maybe, I thought, she deserved a pretty feller, but not Fink, not if he was the rustler boss like I thought he was.

It turned out that after he'd arrived in this country he'd stayed around Nora for a month or two and then had bought the Lazy A ranch from a widow woman who wanted to go home to Kansas City, and ever since had been building up his herd. Esme figured he was running a couple of thousand head. The times he'd visited he'd talked about becoming the biggest rancher within a hundred miles.

"After father died he came over to pay his respects," Esme said. "At the time he said if I wanted to go back to Virginia he might be interested in buying the R Bar, but I told him I was going to stay, at least for a while."

She went on: "I love this country. The air is so clear and dry. You can see for miles. And the mountains are magnificent. I don't think I would ever leave."

She paused a moment. "Unless the rustlers drive me out."

"Esme," I said earnestly. "That ain't never goin' to happen. They've done their best to kill me and failed. Now I'm gonna go after them."

She could see I was beginning to get tired. She reached over and squeezed my hand and looked at me with what I took to be a tender look, then stood.

"You're tired," she said. "Get some sleep. I'll wake you up for supper. Then maybe you can get up if you feel like it."

"Come, Beauty," she said and left, closing the door behind her, and I lay back and dozed off for a few minutes. But I wasn't really sleepy so I lay there letting my thoughts drift back to Ma and those growing up years in the gold camps.

Suddenly I remembered the diary. Now would be a good time to look at it. I sat up and swung my feet over the edge of the bed. Then I tried standing up. The room swam for a minute but it soon steadied down and I took a hesitant step toward the dresser where my clothes were. Once started I knew I had to get there. I'd never live it down if Esme or Mary Lou came into the room and found me lying on the floor in nothing but my shirt.

It taken a minute. I'd take a step and stop and let the room settle down and then take another step. I finally got there, grabbed my clothes, and lurched back to the bed. I pulled on my long johns and then my pants.

Clean clothes next to my skin felt real good, but would have felt better if I could have had a bath. But, dang it, Saturday had come and gone while I was lying there unconscious. Maybe I could get Mary Lou to heat me up a tub of water tomorrow and then if I could keep her and Esme out of the kitchen for a while I'd have me that bath I'd been promising myself.

As soon as I got my jeans on I got my saddlebags and dragged them over by the chair. Sitting down, I fished around and found that diary and opened it up. It was written in longhand and all them loops and curlycues made it hard for me to figure out.

I studied on the first page and finally made out what it said. The first line read:

Geraldine Carmen Groupe Tackett

The "Tackett" had been added in a different color ink. I figured that meant that Ma had been married. That was a relief. A burden lifted off of me that had been there most of my life. After all, a person ought to have a pa he can point to. I wondered why Ma never told me. Maybe she just assumed I knew. I didn't, but whenever I'd thought to ask about where we'd come from, Ma just turned away.

The second line read: Her diary, 1858.

I had just turned to the next page when someone knocked gently on the door.

I stuffed the diary down beside me in the chair. "Come on in," I said. "It's open."

This time it was Mary Lou. "Mr. Tackett," she said. "Miss Esme said to tell you that Mr. Fink has stopped by and she has asked him to stay for supper."

Strange, I thought, that he'd come by just now. Then it hit me. His man up in the valley had found his dead pardner, the one I'd stabbed, but he hadn't found me. They knew I was bad hurt. They knew I'd hired on at the R Bar R, and Fink was here to find out if I'd made my way back here or if the boys were out hunting for me.

I said to Mary Lou, "If you can get her alone you tell Esme not to tell Fink I'm here. You sneak out to the bunkhouse when the boys come in and tell them to keep quiet, too."

Mary Lou went out quietly and closed the door behind her. I looked around for my gun, actually it was the gun of the man I'd killed, and spotted my gun belt, with the gun in the holster, hanging on one of the pegs on the side wall.

I took it down and looked at it carefully for the first time. It was a Colt .45 with plain walnut grips and looked to be in good condition. I fetched a rag from my saddlebags and stripped it and cleaned it. Then I loaded it and shoved it under the pillow where it was hidden, but where I could reach it easy from the chair where I was sitting.

I looked around to see what else needed doing and decided I'd better close the shutters on the windows, just in case Fink or one of his men, if he'd brought any, was nosing around. I found a farmer match on the dresser and lighted the lamp, then I eased over to the windows to take a look-see.

The bedroom was in the back of the house and the one window looked out on the mountains while the other looked to the north with the mountains off to the right and the desert to the left.

The sun going down in the west lighted up the entire western slope of the mountain. I easily made out where the canyons came down but hard as I looked I couldn't find the break in the terrain that would have indicated the lower side of the hidden valley. It was truly hidden by the heavy growth of trees and by the natural formation of the mountain. No wonder the old colonel hadn't known it was there.

Regretfully I closed the shutters, wishing I was outside sitting on the porch steps or maybe currying Old Dobbin. I was glad he'd busted loose and had come back to the ranch. I'd had him for four years and we knew each other's ways. I would have missed him if a mountain lion had gotten him while he was tied up or if something else had happened to him.

I was tired by now, still being weak from loss of blood and the bullet wound, and hungry, too, but I knew food would have to wait until Fink left. I felt my ribs where Sears had kicked me. They were still tender but I figured he hadn't done any real damage since I could breathe without hurting.

I decided not to try to read any more of Ma's diary right then and instead lay down on top of the spread just meaning to rest a few minutes, but no sooner had I hit the pillow than I drifted off to sleep. A gentle tapping on the door awakened me. I reached for the gun under my pillow and put it by my side where it was hidden from anyone coming into the room.

It wasn't necessary. It was Esme who came in when I answered the knock.

"Yeah, I'm awake," I said, before she could ask. "Has yer friend gone?"

She came in and sat down in the chair. I saw her fumbling for something beside her and she came up with Ma's diary.

"What's this?" she asked opening it. Aloud she read, "Geraldine Carmen Groupe Tackett. Her diary, 1858."

She closed it quickly. "Oh, I'm sorry," she said. "It must be your mother's diary. I didn't mean to pry."

"It don't matter," I said. "She must have been educated because she writes in a fancy hand. I have trouble readin' it. I'll figure it out one day when I got more time."

"Maybe I could help," she said.

66

"Maybe you could," I said, "but later. I need to know about Fink. What'd he want?"

"You," she said. "You."

After passing the time of day he told her he'd heard she'd hired a gunslinger named Tackett. He warned her that I had a bad reputation as a known killer and that I likely was wanted in California and Nevada. He suggested that Esme fire me before I created real problems for her and said he'd send a couple of his men over if she needed help. He apparently was not aware that I'd hired Lew and Blackie. They'd gone out yesterday and weren't due back until tomorrow, so he'd missed them.

She told him that I'd only stayed around a few days. That after we'd been shot at I'd taken off, telling her that if she wanted a gunfighter she'd have to pay fighting wages, which she refused to do. She said she'd think about his offer of help.

He told her he'd hired Evan Stevens on at his ranch, but he knew he'd be willing to come back to work at the R Bar. Then he suggested that, what with all the trouble, Esme might reconsider selling out. He also said he thought he was losing a few cattle, too. She thought this was odd because, while she'd mentioned being shot at she had never said anything to him about rustlers or losing cattle.

She said she was still not interested in selling. And, furthermore, she didn't want Stevens coming around under any circumstances.

He took what she said in good humor, talked about things in general for a while, and immediately after dinner mounted up and rode off.

"Del," she said gravely. "There's only one thing that worries me. I think he knew Mary Lou. He said he thought he'd seen her somewhere before. I asked Mary Lou and she doesn't remember him but he might have seen her sometime when he was in town."

About then there was another knock on the door and Mary Lou came in with a huge trayful of food, a plate heaped with beans and beef, and what looked like a third of an apple pie on another plate.

And, of course, a mug of steaming coffee. She'd also made some tortillas and there was half a dozen of them on another dish.

It was late and I was hungry, but I ate slow. Except for that soup at lunch I hadn't had anything to eat for nigh on to five days and a man who eats fast after going hungry that long is likely to regret it. Besides, I wanted to savor every mouthful.

Mary Lou had set down the tray and left, but Beauty had sneaked in behind her and she stayed, paying more attention to the food than to either Esme or me. I figured she'd been fed, but toward the end I slipped her a couple of bites when I thought Esme wasn't looking. A man who likes to eat like I do doesn't like to see anyone or anything else go hungry.

Between bites I asked Esme what happened to the horse I rode in on. She said they hadn't seen it and it probably had headed home. I remembered then that's after I'd ridden out of the canyon he'd tried to veer south.

"Likely went back to the Lazy A," I said. He was a spotted gelding and I think I'll know him if I see him again."

After I finished eating Esme took the tray and started to leave.

"You get some sleep," she said, "and I'll see you in the morning. Come along, Beauty."

Beauty wagged her tail, but didn't move.

"Be all right if she stayed the night?" I asked.

"Of course," she smiled, and went out, closing the door behind her.

I took off my jeans and shirt, but you can bet I kept my long johns on, blew out the lamp and went over and opened the shutters. That fresh air smelled good. I taken a couple of deep breaths then went back and climbed into bed.

Man could get used to this, I thought, sleepin' in a soft bed, bein' waited on hand and foot by a couple of pretty women, havin' your faithful dog with you and knowin' your faithful horse is just outside in the barn.

Next thing I knew it was morning.

CHAPTER 6

Lying there in that big old bed with Beauty sprawled across the bottom and still snoring, I felt good. The ache in my head was almost gone and that big supper last night had begun to put some strength back in my arms and legs.

"Come on, Beauty, it's time to get up," I said, sitting up and swinging my feet onto the floor. I dressed quickly and walked, still a little unsteady, out to the kitchen. Mary Lou was there building a fire in the cookstove.

"Good morning," she said. "Breakfast in half an hour."

I was carrying my saddlebags and gun belt and I went on out to the bunkhouse and tossed them on my bunk, along with my bedroll which someone had taken off of Old Dobbin and brought inside.

I went outside to the tin basin, filled it with water, and soaped my face up good and then shaved off that five-day growth of beard. I have a dark, heavy beard anyway and it didn't want to come off. In some places I took chunks of skin, in others I left clumps of whisker. Shaving without a mirror sure ain't the easiest thing, but finally I finished and even though I was oozing blood here and there I felt better.

Blackie and Lew were still out on the range, but Billy Bob was already in the kitchen when I got there and so was Esme.

"Need a favor," I said to her. "If I could get a tub of hot water today I'd surely like to take a bath. I must be smellin' like a boar pig. I'd consider it a real favor."

"Now you know why we've all been sittin' upwind from ya," Billy

Bob laughed. A body oughtn't to take offense at the truth, so I didn't.

Esme said she thought the hot water could be arranged.

"And maybe you ladies could stay out of the kitchen for a little bit?" I asked.

Esme said she thought that could be arranged, too.

But after breakfast, when Mary Lou was putting big kettles of water on the stove to heat, Esme beckoned me to follow her. We went down the hall that led to the bedrooms. She stopped at the end and opened a door I hadn't paid much attention to earlier. There was a small window high up in the wall and by its light I saw a real bathtub, big enough to sit in. On closer look I saw that it even had a drain that apparently led to the outside.

I just stared. It had been over a year since I'd been in a hotel with a real bathtub. Ordinarily I got a bath by standing in a washtub and pouring water over me or else found me a stream.

"Father grew up in the city and never got over liking all the comforts of home," Esme said. "That's why he put the pump and wetsink in the kitchen and the bathtub here. He had it brought by wagon overland from Kansas City."

"Might take me two baths to get clean," I said.

There was soap on a ledge and a big heavy towel hanging on a hook. I was feeling strong enough to fetch the hot water and as soon as Esme turned away I shut the door, stripped off my clothes, and climbed in. An hour later I came out of that bathroom a new man, ready to whistle and sing or fight the devil hisself.

First thing Billy Bob said when he saw me was, "Don't ferget, Del, too much bathin'll weakin' ya."

I knew it would be a few days before I got my strength back and I decided it would be smart to take it easy before tackling Fink and his outfit, being convinced, as I was, that they were the source of our trouble. I loafed around most of the day, curried Old Dobbin and played a bit with Beauty, throwing sticks for her to fetch and rubbing her belly when she turned on her back, which she liked to do.

First, however, I suggested to Billy Bob that he should ride south a few miles then head east toward Sweetwater Canyon, the south-ernmost of Early Mountain's three canyons.

"Just do a little scoutin' around," I told him. "See if anything seems different or unusual and keep an eye out for trouble as well as R Bar cows.

"I wouldn't go up the canyon if I was you. If there's an easy way to that hidden valley they'll have a man there and you'll be a sittin' duck."

After he'd gone I found the women and took them out to do a little target shooting with rifles and pistols both. Billy Bob had done what I asked and had a couple of practice sessions with them, but I wanted to make sure they could handle them. I didn't like leaving them alone at the ranch but I knew there would be times when I had no choice. Most Western girls grew up knowing about guns but Esme was from genteel Virginia and Mary Lou was a farmer's girl out of Illinois. Neither one was any Annie Oakley.

Lew and Blackie rode in in the late afternoon. They'd been gone for three days, riding a wide semicircle around the ranch on the desert side, and pushing any cattle they found up toward the mountains. For a ranch that was supposed to have about 3000 head they'd found mighty few, but thought most of them had already headed for the hills of their own accord. They also re-ported that two of the water holes still had water, but figured they'd be dry in another week or two unless there was rain.

"Have any trouble findin' them?" I asked.

"Nah," Lew replied. "Billy Bob told us about where they was, then when we thought we were close we followed a few animal tracks and when we sighted the bees they led us right to it."

One thing about dry country, if there's water the wild animals and the bees will know where it is. More than one desert man would have died of thirst if he hadn't known this and followed the bees to where the water was.

I heard tell once of a man who'd run out of water and was stumbling down a dry wash on his last legs, leading his horse which about as weak as he was. Unexpected like he came across a porcupine clawing a hole in what appeared to be dry sand. He managed to drive the animal off and discovered the bottom of the hole was damp. He started digging with his knife and another foot down water started seeping in. Waiting around for nearly a day he got enough water for himself and his horse. As he was leaving he noticed the porcupine headed for the hole. It had been waiting all that time for him to go.

Night came and Billy Bob still hadn't come in. I was worried. I cussed myself for sending him out alone, but he was an old hand and I'd figured he could take care of himself, even if he had only one arm.

But a lot could happen to a man alone in these vast and empty Western lands. His horse could break a leg and strand him miles from the nearest water or ranch. He could be bit by a rattler or gored or trampled by a wild steer, which is about as dangerous as any animal around. Or being careless or unlucky he could come across some unfriendly Indians.

I slept in the bunkhouse that night with one ear cocked for Billy Bob, but he didn't come in. Come dawn I rousted the boys out, told Blackie to stay at the ranch, and, without waiting for breakfast, Lew and I saddled up and headed in the direction Billy Bob had taken a day earlier.

Once we were away from the ranch it wasn't long before we found his tracks and we set off following them at a fast trot. It was a cool morning with only a hint of the hot summer days ahead and not a cloud anywhere. By the time the sun came up over Early Mountain we were already five miles south of the ranch and turning to follow Billy Bob's tracks almost due east toward the entrance to Sweetwater Canyon. In the daylight we could see scattered cattle grazing peacefully.

Trouble was, one of them turned out to be a horse, instead, and he had a saddle on him and his reins were dragging.

He stood still while we cantered up to him. There wasn't any doubt that it was Billy Bob's horse and Billy Bob's saddle. I swore and Lew swore and reached down and took the horse's reins. We set off again heading toward Sweetwater Canyon. Overhead Lew spotted some buzzards cirling near the head of the canyon. We both knew what that meant and we took off running.

We might as well have walked for all the good it did us. Billy Bob was lying where he'd fallen off his horse. You could see he hadn't moved and there were bloodstains on his leather vest. I turned him over and there were two bullet holes in the left side of his chest, no more than an inch apart. Whoever had shot him wasn't no amateur. His six-gun was still in its holster with the thong fastened over the grip. It was plain he hadn't been expecting any trouble.

While I was looking at Billy Bob, Lew had been looking for sign. He beckoned me over.

"Look here," he said. "Another horse has been here. Looks like him and Billy Bob stopped to talk. They probably knew each other."

"If that's the case he probably sucker shot Billy Bob when he wasn't payin' attention. Just plain cold-blooded murder," I said.

"He wasn't in no hurry to leave, neither," Lew said. "See here where he turned his horse and just walked him away. You want me to go after him?"

"Probably not a good idea," I said. "Whoever he is has at least a day's head start. But take a good look at those hoof tracks, I want to recognize 'em if we see 'em again."

We histed Billy Bob's body up and laid it face down across his saddle and tied it on. There was a sadness on me and an anger rising in me. This was a good old man. And he'd stayed by Esme when the going was rough. Now he was dead, shot down in cold blood without a chance.

Before we put him on the horse I went through his pockets. Wasn't much there. A couple of silver dollars and a Barlow folding knife. There was a letter tucked in an inside vest pocket. I handed it to Lew, casual-like.

"Take a look," I said. "What's it say?"

He looked at me kind of funny. "It's addressed to a Mr. William

R. Doyle," he said, looking at the envelope, "from someone named Elizabeth Doyle. It's postmarked Abilene, Texas."

He took the letter out of the envelope and began reading.

Dear Father:

I am so hoping you can come visit me this summer. School will be out on June 1 and my little charges will be out of my hair until September. Seriously, I have really enjoyed teaching this year. And unless I'm lucky and Prince Charming comes along I'll probably wind up as an old maid schoolteacher. I hope not. In the meantime I have nothing to do for three months unless I can find a temporary job as a clerk or a waitress. Regardless, I do want to see you, so please come.

Your loving daughter,

It was signed "Liddy."

"Must be Billy Bob's pet name for her," he said, handing the letter back to me.

I taken it and put it in my pocket. I'd give it to Esme when we got back to the ranch and she would have to write the sad news to Elizabeth Doyle. I didn't envy her the task.

It wasn't yet noon when we trotted up to the R Bar R. Blackie had been out spading up a plot for a kitchen garden. He came over and helped Lew unload Billy Bob's remains while I went on up to the house. Esme answered my knock.

"Back so soon?" she asked, then saw my face. "What is it? What's wrong?"

"It's Billy Bob. He's been shot dead. We found him up toward the mouth of Sweetwater Canyon."

She turned white and put a hand to her breast. "Billy Bob. Oh, no!" she gasped.

Her face kind of crumpled up and the tears began running down her cheeks. I took her arm and led her over to one of the chairs on the veranda and she sank into it. After a moment she got ahold of herself.

"I can't believe it," she said. "He was such a nice man. He wouldn't harm anybody. Who would want to kill him?"

"I don't know," I said, "but I sure aim to find out."

"How did it happen?" she asked.

"He was shot twice in the chest up close. Looks like it was someone he knowed. He didn't even try to draw his gun."

I handed her the letter. She took it silently and read it. More tears appeared at the corners of her eyes, but she didn't cry.

"I didn't even know he had a daughter. He never talked much about himself. Oh, dear. Oh, dear. I will have to write a letter to her right away and one of you will have to go to town to mail it."

They had buried Esme's father off to the side of the house and had fenced the grave in to keep the varmints out. We wrapped Billy Bob in a blanket and buried him alongside the old colonel. Blackie had made a crude wooden cross and had written on it

William R. Doyle
Killed near here 1888

I didn't know much about the Good Book, not being able to read all that well, but we all bowed our heads and I said a few words, asking the Lord to look after his soul. Then we went up to the house where Mary Lou had fixed some lunch.

After we ate Esme spoke up. "Maybe it would be best if I sold out to Reggie Fink and went on back to Virginia. Father was killed here and now Billy Bob. Someone has shot at our hands and run them off and you've almost been killed. I don't want any other deaths on my hands."

The rest of us kind of shuffled uneasily in our chairs. I looked at Mary Lou and she was pale. If Esme left she'd be alone and penniless again. With Lew and Blackie it was different. They'd just mount up and drift again until they could find another job. In the meantime, if they had to they could live off the country or else ride the grub line, or both.

It was the same way with me, but I was damned if I wanted to run away from a fight, not if it meant letting Billy Bob's killer go free. Especially since I had a hunch I knew who had killed him.

I spoke up. "None of us here have any right to tell you what you oughta do, Esme. But I hope you won't act hasty-like. If you sell out now whoever is responsible for killin' Billy Bob and rustlin' your cows is gonna get away with it. I don't think you want that and I sure don't either. You got to write Billy Bob's girl. You gonna tell her we're not gonna do nuthin' about catchin' his killer?"

"We could send for the sheriff," Esme replied.

"The sheriff is seventy miles away and has problems of his own. You might as well face it. There ain't no law up here unless we bring it ourselves. And I intend to do just that, beginnin' today."

"I don't want you killed, too," she whispered.

"Me, neither," I said. I turned to Blackie and Lew. "You two willin' to stay on?"

"Ain't nobody runnin' us off," Lew said and Blackie nodded in agreement.

"Thank you. All three of you," Esme said in a low voice.

I stood up and headed for the door with Blackie and Lew right behind me.

"I got me a idea," I said when we were outside.

I stayed around the ranch until the sun had set behind the desert then I mounted Old Dobbin and headed once again for Early Mountain. During the afternoon I'd cleaned my guns and had Mary Lou pack me food enough for a couple of days on the trail. Esme came to the door as I swung into the saddle.

"Be careful, Del," she said. "And come back."

She said something else that sounded like, "I need you," but I knew I'd heard wrong so I kept on going. This time, instead of heading for one of the canyons I struck farther north, aiming to go around the north shoulder of the mountain and find the trail into the valley that had been blocked off with the barbed wire. There was nearly a full moon which made it easy to see. I rode until I could no longer see the dark bulk of the mountain on my right, then I turned and headed east until once again I could see the north side of the mountain. I rode down into a little hollow and made camp. There were clumps of grass there and I staked Old Dobbin out so he could graze during the night. I unrolled my bedroll and using my saddle as a pillow I lay back to contemplate. But I'd hardly begun when I fell off to sleep. It had been a long day and I still didn't have my strength back. I'd removed the bandage on my head in the afternoon but it was still scabby and sore. The ache, however, had finally gone away, at least most of the time.

It was full daylight before I awoke. I shook out my boots to make sure no scorpions or other varmints had crawled in during the night and pulled them on. I dearly wanted a cup of coffee but I decided against building a fire and took a long drink of water instead. I poured some more in my hat and let Old Dobbin have a drink, then I saddled up and rode out of the hollow and toward the foot of Early Mountain.

In the darkness of last night I'd come to the point where the mountain turned so that I would be skirting it east and west instead of north and south. In the daylight I could see that there was another range of mountains behind Early Mountain, but I wasn't interested in them now. I wanted to find a trail up Early and into the hidden valley.

The slope of the mountain here on its north side was more gentle than it was on its western face and I headed Old Dobbin up the slope until I was riding in the first scattering of pine and fir.

Only then did I head east, riding in and out among the trees where it would be harder to spot me if anybody came along down below.

I didn't expect anyone, but I'd gotten careless once before up here and I wasn't going to let it happen again.

It was midmorning before I found what I was looking for. Cow tracks, a lot of them, headed down the mountain. I'd just come over a low hump in the terrain that was barely high enough to hide any cattle from the view looking east from where I was or any point lower down. None of the tracks looked fresh which meant that they hadn't moved any cattle out of the valley since the day I'd been shot, at least.

I stifled an impulse to see where the trail led and turned Old Dobbin up the slope toward the valley. It was slow going because I kept to one side of the trail, not knowing what or who I might run into as I got close to that barbed wire barrier.

When I figured it wasn't too far off, I dismounted and tied Old Dobbin loosely to a small tree, taken my moccasins from a saddlebag and changed into them. Then I eased through the trees, stopping every few feet to listen. By now the trees were so thick you could only see a few feet ahead. I'd been climbing steadily for nearly an hour before I spotted the wire. In fact, I was almost on top of it before I saw it. I spent another fifteen minutes dodging from tree to tree looking for some indication of life.

At one point I recognized the deadfall where I'd tried to hide and where I'd killed the rustler. Someone had found him and taken him away, but there'd been no rain since then and there were still some visible brown spots on the dead leaves that I took to be blood.

I hurried back to Old Dobbin and rode him up the trail to the wire and then tethered him off to one side in the trees. I wanted him close in case I had to take off from there in a hurry.

The valley seemed quiet and peaceful and here and there steers and cows grazed calmly across the valley floor. One steer was close enough so I could read his brand. It didn't surprise me none to find that it read R Bar R.

The slope bounding the upper side of the valley was a steep one and heavily forested. It made a natural barrier for keeping the cattle on the valley floor. Keeping to the trees I had skirted the valley on the high side for more than half its length when I spotted the log cabin. It was small and I guessed it didn't have more than one room. It had no windows in the side I was looking at or in the back. When I reached the far side I saw that there was a lean-to built out from the cabin wall and beyond it a small corral with two horses in it. Under the shed roof of the lean-to a saddled horse was tied.

Looked to me like there was two men in the cabin. One had ridden the saddled horse up here this morning. The other two horses belonged to the man who was stationed here. I knew now what I had to do. One reason I'd come up here was to put these crooks out of business. And there wasn't any better time to begin than now.

CHAPTER 7

I TOOK A CAREFUL look around. There wasn't anything in sight except the horses and some cattle grazing around the valley. I injunned down to the back of the cabin and then along the opposite side from the lean-to, not wanting to startle the horses.

At the corner of the cabin I stopped and peered around the front. There was nobody there. Quietly I moved to the cabin's only window and sneaked a quick look inside. There were two men sitting at a table drinking coffee. One of them was Evan Stevens. I ducked down quickly and moved in a crouch to the door. It was open just a crack.

I drew my gun, shoved the door open, and stepped inside. They looked up startled and Stevens started to reach for his gun. Then he saw that mine was pointed right at him and he sank back in his chair.

"Howdy, fellers," I said pleasantly.

Stevens uttered an oath and then just sat there glaring at me. The other man, a stocky puncher with black hair and a mean look on his thin-lipped mouth, grunted.

"You," he said, "I knowed I should have plugged ya again after Joe shot ya."

"Don't let it bother ya. We all make mistakes," I said.

"We sure do," a voice behind me said as the barrel of a gun poked me in the small of my back.

"Now drop your gun," the voice said, "and move over there by the table."

I did as I was told, dropping my gun to the floor and moving over to the table. I turned around slowly.

The man with the gun was about thirty-five years old, with dark wavy hair and startling blue eyes. He wasn't as big as me, just a mite under six feet, I judged, and lean. I knew who he was without asking but I asked anyway.

"You're Fink?"

"That's right," he smiled, showing even, white teeth, "and you're Sackett."

In spite of his gun I almost went after him right there.

"Tackett," I said grimly. "With a T."

He laughed. "I'll remember to tell them that when they're carving your tombstone."

He turned to Stevens and the other puncher. "You and Dave have been loafing long enough. I sent Harry and Frank down to the south end to begin pushing the cattle up to the north. I've got a buyer waiting in Chambers and I've promised him a minimum of five hundred head. I told him I'd have them there in a week."

"What're we gonna to do with this galoot?" Dave asked, jerking a thumb at me.

"I know what I'm going to do," Stevens snarled, and before I could move he'd backhanded me a good one across the face, bloodying my lips with his knuckles.

I just looked at him. "Brave, ain't ya," I said, spitting blood on the dirt floor of the cabin.

"We'll see who's brave before I'm through with you," he said, coming at me again.

He drew back his fist and I braced myself for what I knew was coming. But before he could hit me, Fink stopped him.

"Cut it out, Evan. There'll be time for that later. Let's get the cattle down to the north end of the valley, then you can come back and play with him all you want before you kill him.

"Turn around," he said to me.

I turned around. The next thing I felt was a smashing blow on the back of my head. After that I didn't feel anything for a long time.

When I came to the western sun was shining through the cabin door and into my eyes. I'd been out for several hours. I lifted my head and quickly put it back down. It was one big throb. I went to move my hands and discovered I couldn't. They were tied behind my back. I lay there a minute trying to figure out what had happened. Then I remembered.

In my eagerness to capture Stevens and Dave I'd forgotten a basic rule: Always watch your back. And Fink, who must have gone out to check the horses while I was on the other side of the cabin, had come back and found me there. He must have hit me on the head with the butt of his gun to make it easier to tie me up. I tried to move my legs only to find they were tied together, too. They hadn't hogtied me, though. They'd been in too big a hurry to get the cattle rounded up and pushed down to the north end of the valley befor dark.

A sudden wave of panic went through me. When they had rounded up the cattle Stevens was coming back to kill me. I had to get away and I didn't have much time.

I was lying on my side facing the cabin door. If only I could get at that hideout knife I carried. I knew they hadn't found it because I could feel its haft pressing against the inside of my calves which were pulled tight together by the ropes around my ankles.

I bent my legs up behind me and arched my back, reaching down as far as I could. I couldn't even come close. That knife might as well have been in China for all the good it was going to do me. I stretched as far as I could, but I was just wasting my time and I knew it.

I remembered a skinny cowboy I'd known once who had a trick he used to make money with. He'd bet you five bucks or fifty that with his hands tied behind his back he could pull them over his legs and bring them around in front of him. I tried that, too, and after a couple of minutes decided I'd have to find another way to make money or save my life.

Desperately I looked around the room. There was nothing I could use to cut the ropes. I couldn't burn them off because the fire was out. I spied my gun over in a corner where they'd kicked it but it wouldn't do me any good until I got loose—if I got loose. I strained at my bonds, but whoever had tied me knew what he was doing. I was tied tight and I couldn't reach the knot with my fingers.

This is it, I thought. I'm a dead man. And I never got done what I'd set out to do. I'd never even read Ma's diary.

For sure now, Esme would lose the ranch. Mary Lou, who was a sweet girl, but weak, would likely wind up back at Nora's where she'd either put up with or get beat up by people like Evan Stevens. Lew and Blackie would drift along and before the year was up Reggie Fink would have moved onto the R Bar R, maybe even forced Esme to marry him.

I started struggling again, straining at the ropes until my wrists were rubbed raw and there was sweat standing out on my forhead. It was no use.

I had finally given up and was lying there panting, when a shadow fell across my face. My heart sank. I knew it was Evan Stevens and after he'd finished kicking me around—playing with me, Fink had said—he'd kill me. And there'd be no tombstone that said Tackett or Sackett or anything else, just a shallow grave in a hidden valley.

Didn't matter much I thought. There wasn't anyone to miss me, no wife, no kinfolk. I was like a pebble someone dropped in a pool. I'd made a few ripples in my time but they'd quickly be forgotten and so would I.

"Dang it, Tackett, you kin shore get yerself into a peck of trouble," Jack Sears said.

He stood there grinning down at me a moment then he reached into his pocket with his left hand and pulled out a big old Barlow folding knife. Stuck it under his right arm and held it tightly there while he opened the blade with the fingers of his left hand.

"If you hadn't broke my hand I could do this a lot easier," he grumbled.

Taking the knife in his left hand he leaned over suddenly and for a flash I thought maybe this was get even time for Jack Sears. But, instead, he reached behind me and sliced the rope binding my hands and a second later did the same on the rope tied around my feet.

I sat up and chafed my wrists with hands that had gone numb from being tied too tightly.

"They'll be comin' back any minute." I said. "Let's get out of here."

I went over to the corner and picked up my gun and shoved it in its holster, stuck my hat on my head, and headed for the door. Sears was already outside but he wasn't moving.

"Somebody comin'," he said.

I looked off to the north and in the distance I could see a horseman headed in our direction.

"That's gotta be Stevens comin' back to kill me."

"You gonna fight or run?" Sears asked.

"Fight," I said, flexing the fingers on my right hand. They were still a little numb and my head was pounding like a triphammer.

Hugging the wall of the cabin we eased back around the corner and under the lean-to. While we waited for the horseman I asked Sears what he was doing there.

"Just curious," he said. "I been campin' down there in the canyon waitin' for my hand to heal so's I can kill ya. And these fellers keep ridin' in and out, along that trail where I found you the last time you got your head in the way of somethin' hard.

"I been in a cave over on the other side of the canyon and they ain't seen me. I guess they wasn't lookin' for no one to be there.

"Anyway, after that wavy-haired feller went up there today I decided to follow him, only on foot, so in case someone come along I could duck into the rocks.

"By the time I got up here they'd come and gone, or so I figured, since there wasn't no horses around the cabin, which you can see plain from where the trail comes into the valley."

"You saved my life," I said. "Matter of fact, that's twice you could have killed me."

"Thought about it," he admitted. "But it wouldn't be no fun with you beat up and tied up and all. I kin wait until your head is well and my hand is workin' again."

I took a quick look around the corner of the cabin. The horseman was only about a hundred yards away by now and I could see it was Stevens. He loped up to the cabin and swung down, ground-hitching his horse. He went into the cabin and we could hear as he began cursing. As he came running out the door I stepped out in front of the cabin.

"Stevens," I said.

He swung around, saw me, and went for his gun, and he was fast. But mine seemed to leap into my hand and I lifted it up, pointed it right at him, and squeezed the trigger. He'd already fired, but he was in too big a hurry and his first bullet hit the ground in front of me, kicking up dust. My bullet hit him in the left shoulder and he flinched, which caused his second shot to go wide. I walked toward him, firing as I went. He jerked as my second bullet hit him in the chest and he dropped his gun. I shot him a third time and he tottered backwards and fell in a heap.

I walked over to him and looked down. He didn't say anything because he was dead.

"Some shootin'," Sears said at my elbow. "Them shots should bring the rest of that gang a-runnin'. I ain't much good shootin' left-handed so let's get out of here."

Stevens' horse, frightened by the noise of the shooting, had trotted off fifty or so yards, but he stood still while Sears went over to him. Sears threw the reins over his head and climbed awkwardly into the saddle.

"See ya," he said, kicking the horse in its flanks and heading off across the valley at a trot.

I started to holler at him, but decided it wasn't any use. And, what the hell, he didn't owe me. In fact, I owed him. A lot. My life.

I went back to Stevens, stripped his gun belt from him, and buckled it around my hips. I picked up his gun and put it in its holster. Next, I went back in the cabin for a quick look around. Then, without a backward glance I headed for the woods behind the cabin and went straight up the mountain. I figured Fink and his men, if they'd heard the shooting and decided to come back, would think I would try to get out of the valley and head for the R Bar.

I climbed until the trees began to thin out, then headed south until I found what I was looking for, a large rock that would protect me from the wind. I crawled behind it, piled up some leaves, burrowed into them, and went to sleep. Tomorrow I would try to figure out what my next step was.

I woke up in the first light of morning to an aching head. Reaching back I found a lump the size of a hen's egg. Fortunately for me my hat had cushioned the blow a little, or I might still be lying back there in the cabin with Evan Stevens waiting for me to come to so he could gloat over me before he killed me.

Lying there, I tried to figure out Jack Sears. He didn't make much sense to me. I had beaten him up and shamed him in front of half the town of Nora. I'd busted his hand, dunked him in the horse trough, and run him out of town. Not only that but I'd killed three of his kinfolk who were trying to hold up the wagon I was guarding. Seemed to me like he had a right to hold a grudge.

But he'd come upon me twice when I was helpless and both times he'd let me go. Once he'd even helped me escape. Both times he'd said he wanted to kill me in a fair fight once his hand was healed. But I couldn't fight him now—no way. I owed him my life, so I couldn't take his. But, still, I didn't want him taking mine, either.

Well, hell, one problem at a time, and Reggie Fink and his gang of rustlers were my first problem. If I lived through that I'd worry about Sears. Until then, I'd try to stay out of his way, unless, of course, I needed him to get me out of trouble again.

Trouble. That seemed to be my middle name these days, and maybe my first and last names, as well. Twice I'd left my backside unguarded and twice I'd paid dearly for it. Third time I might be even unluckier.

Still in all, I was evening the odds a mite. I'd killed the one rustler with my knife and I'd won a shootout with Evan Stevens, a dangerous man, all right, but not quite dangerous enough.

First thing I had to do was to get back to Old Dobbin. I just hoped Fink or one of his men hadn't found him. Getting back to the ranch on foot would be a long day's walk, maybe two.

I'd have to be careful heading back to the north end of the valley. I still didn't know if the rustlers had heard the shooting and had gone back and found Stevens dead. If they had, they'd be looking for me. Before I'd left the cabin I'd looked around to see if there was any food I could take with me. There was a pot of beans on the stove, but I had nothing to carry them in. I'd found a hunk of bread and a can of peaches. I'd stuffed them in a sack and brought them along.

Not having eaten since yesterday morning, I was powerfully hungry. I ate the bread and then, using my knife as a can opener, I got at those peaches. They tasted good. Thing I missed most was coffee. I figured that would have to wait until I got back to the ranch.

I'd headed south the night before, so now I doubled back on myself, moving cautiously along the side of Early Mountain and keeping a careful eye out. But I figured that up here I was pretty safe. If those rustlers were typical cowboys, they wouldn't go hunting me on foot and the side of that mountain was too steep and too wooded for easy riding. On the other hand, supposing there was a real woodsman among them?

It took me most of the morning to get to the north end of the valley and I was still high up, maybe half a mile above the spot where the valley broke off and the trail down along the mountain's north side began. With any luck I'd be on Old Dobbin and headed back to the ranch in another hour.

I was leery now and I went down the mountain like a ghost, moving from tree to tree and careful not to step on a stick or a twig, anything that might make a cracking noise.

Noise! I stopped dead still behind a big fir. There was no noise.

No birds singing. Nothing. Something had frightened them. Was it me? Or was it someone else?

I eased down on my stomach and carefully inched around that tree, scanning every foot of the slope in front of me. Nothing. I squirmed back behind the tree and lay there trying not to breathe. My heart was beating fast and I was sweating, partly from the long hike on a warm day and partly because I was scared. There was something or somebody out there, I could feel it.

It's hard to spot a man who isn't moving. It's movement that catches the eye. The Indians knew that, especially the Apaches, who maybe were the greatest guerrilla fighters in history. On occasion they'd lie right out in the open without moving and more than one battle-wise Indian fighter had lost his life because he saw them too late.

The trouble with the white man is he gets impatient. The Indian will wait all day; he's got no place to go and nothing to do when he gets there except wait until it's time to fight again. Well, I wasn't no Indian, but long ago I'd learned the value of patience.

The woods were absolutely quiet except for a fly that buzzed around me now and then. He was a nuisance but he did one thing for me; he kept me awake. I don't know how long I lay there, but I was beginning to think I'd been imagining things when suddenly I heard a voice calling low to someone.

"Jeb?"

"Yeah?"

"Don't look like he's comin', does it?"

"Well, if he was, you done scared him off."

"He's still gotta get his horse."

"No he don't. He coulda got out of here on Stevens' horse. Then he could circle around and try pickin' up that nag of his by comin' up from down below."

"Slim'll nail him if he does."

"Let's hope yer right. That Sackett or Tackett or whatever he calls hisself is a might tough hombre."

They quit talking but they'd already told me everything I needed to know, where they were and the fact that some puncher called Slim was hidden out by Old Dobbin, waiting for me in case I came up the back way.

I decided I wasn't going to go around the back way. It would mean crossing the open valley, working my way down Greentree Canyon and on around to the north side of the mountain. It would be tomorrow sometime before I reached the spot where I'd left Old Dobbin, and a lot of that time I'd be a sitting duck to Slim or anyone else hiding in the rocks.

I had a better idea. There wasn't much chance of me sneaking by Jeb and his pardner there in the woods, but like I said, I'm a patient man and I could wait until dark, or until one of them gave up. I eased back up the mountain another fifty or so feet where I found a little hollow and I snuggled down in there and took me a nap. I didn't figure those fellers were going anywhere right away. If I was wrong, it didn't make any difference, because I wasn't moving until it was dark. Then I could make my way around them and after that there was only one man, Slim, between me and Old Dobbin. And I was ready, in fact I was eager to take him on. I was getting tired of Fink and his men giving me a bad time. It was my turn now.

It was still light when I awoke. I shook the cobwebs out of my head, taken a swallow of water from my canteen, and crawled back down to that big fir tree, where I had a chance to see Jeb and his pardner if they decided to move out. It wasn't long before Jeb stood up and stretched. I could see him through the branches and I ached to take a shot at him but I figured a shot would bring Slim on the run and in case I missed Jeb I wasn't anxious to take on the three of them.

After he stretched, Jeb called over to his pardner. "Hey, Hank. That feller ain't comin'. If'n he was he'd a been here by now. I think we ought to call it a day."

Hank stood up, too, and I could make him out also through the shadows. He was about thirty feet to one side of Jeb. To my disappointment he wasn't in a mood to leave.

"Fink ain't gonna like it if we show up without his scalp," he said. "I think I'll stay fer a while."

"Tell ya what," Jeb said. "I'll ride down and check in on Slim. If Tackett ain't come up that way, I vote we take his horse and me and Slim'll head for the herd. If you wanna you hang around here for a while and then go lay for him at the foot of the trail. He's gotta come out of here sometime, if he hasn't already, and mebbe you can get yourself a scalp. Man on foot oughtta be easy to bag on the flatland."

"Suit yerself," Hank replied. "I'll lay up here 'til dark, then I'll take the Middleton Canyon trail down to the flatland and wait 'til morning. If he's out there I shouldn't have much trouble spottin' him. If he ain't, well, like you say, he's gotta come outta here sometime."

Jeb turned and tromped off through the woods and toward the cattle trail that led down the side of the mountain.

That decided me. There was a horse down there that I could use in the worst way and I was determined to get him. But there was a man between me and that horse and I was going to have to get him, too, and do it without firing a shot that would be sure to bring Jeb and Slim on the run. I reached down and patted my leg. My knife was still there.

Carefully I eased my way back up the mountain until I was sure I was out of sight of the man called Hank. Then I moved north along the side of the mountain a hundred yards and headed back downhill until I came to the cattle trail. I was now on the north, downhill side of the barbed wire fence. I ducked across the trail and made my way silently to the fence. The wires had been taken down and pulled to one side to let the cattle through. And there not fifty feet away was Hank's horse, tied to a small tree. Hank couldn't be more than a hundred feet up ahead.

I went down on my belly and slowly and silently wiggled forward, moving aside any dead branches or twigs that might make a warning noise if one broke under the weight of my hands or body. Then I spotted him. He was lying on his belly, facing up the mountain where he figured I would be coming from, if I came at all. I reached down and taken my knife from its scabbard and put it between my teeth. I'd crawled within ten feet of him when I realized he was asleep. Waiting all day in warm weather can make a body sleepy. But I'd taken my nap knowing that Hank and Jeb weren't hunting me but instead were just hoping I'd come by.

I stuck my knife back in its scabbard and drew my gun. I was almost on top of him before he sensed my presence and began to move. By then it was too late. I fetched him across his skull with the butt end of my gun. He sank back without making a sound.

At the last minute I'd changed my mind. It wasn't in me to kill a man from behind, unless I had no other choice. In my life I'd already killed more men than I was comfortable about. I rolled him over and looked at him. He wasn't anyone I'd seen before. If he was lucky I wouldn't ever see him again.

I taken his gun and cartridge belt and buckled them around my hips. I went over him for other weapons and found a folding knife in his pocket and took that, too. Then I pulled his boots off—he wasn't wearing no socks—and ran them about a hundred feet up the mountain and threw them as far as I could in opposite directions. He was going to have a long, hard walk to wherever it was he wanted to go.

When I came back, I figured, Oh, what the hell! so I pulled off his pants and long johns and threw them fifteen feet up in a nearby tree. Figured that might be enough to make a hermit out of him. Then I went over and climbed on his horse and headed down the cattle trail, feeling pretty good for a change.

CHAPTER 8

The sun was low in the west and throwing a golden glow over the floor of the valley before I found the trail that led down through Middleton Canyon. By the time I'd gone a little way down the canyon the long shadows had begun to darken it, although, when I turned in my saddle the side of Early Mountain was still bathed in sunlight.

I rode cautiously until I reached the meadow where Jack Sears had found me. It seemed like a year ago even though it had been just a few days. On an impulse, I turned the horse and headed him across the little stream that ran through the canyon and then toward the base of the cliff where Jack Sears had said he was holed up in a cave. It was dark now and I walked the horse slowly, not wanting to make a lot of noise.

All of a sudden I smelled the smoke of a camp fire and then through the trees I caught a flicker of light. When I was about 50 feet away I hollered, "Hello the camp! Can I come in."

"Come on in but keep yer hands in sight," Jack Sears shouted back.

I rode on into the light of the camp fire. There was a coffeepot sitting on a rock next to the fire and a kettle that looked like it had beans in it hanging over the fire, suspended on a steel rod that was supported on each end by a forked stick Sears had driven into the ground. Sears himself was nowhere to be seen.

"Come on out," I said. "I'm harmless. Was just hopin' you could spare a cup of coffee."

Sears eased out into the light of the camp fire, holding a six-gun in his left hand. "Light and set," he said, "but don't try nothin' funny. I shoot pretty straight with my left hand."

I swung down, tied the horse to a tree branch, went over and picked up a tin cup that was sitting by the fire and poured me a cup of coffee. It tasted terrible, but it was coffee and I drank half of it before I set the cup down.

"I see you got away," Sears said.

"You got good eyesight," I replied.

"Have any trouble?"

"Had to steal a horse."

His hand was still in the sling but I noticed he was flexing his fingers.

"How's the hand?" I asked.

"Gettin' better," he said. "I figure in about a month I'll be ready to kill ya."

"I won't fight ya," I said. "You saved my life. I won't fight ya."

"Then I'll shoot ya down like a dog."

"I'll worry about that when the time comes," I said.

"Look," he said. "I got to kill ya. You killed my kinfolk but they was askin' for it and I kin forgive ya fer that. But back there in Nora you shamed me in front of half the town. You sucker punched me and whupped me good witout ever drawin' yer gun or lettin' me fight back.

"You shamed me and I cain't let that pass. I got to kill ya."

"It's up to you," I said. "But look, yer living like a hermit or a Injun or worse out here. And yer havin' to drink that lousy coffee ya make. Whyn't you come back to the R Bar R with me. I got a couple of women there that I don't like leavin' alone. And I gotta take my hands and go after them cattle Fink and his boys stole. They'd feed ya and give ya a place to sleep 'til yer hand heals and you kin watch over 'em."

"I ain't lookin' for no favors, especially from you," he said.

"You'd be doin' me a favor," I said. "Besides, you'll know right where I am when yer ready to start shootin'."

"I ain't much fer cookin'," he admitted. "And yer right, the coffee ain't fit to drink. So I guess I'll ride in with ya."

"But that don't change nothin," he added.

His horse and a packhorse were tethered back in the trees. He fetched them and I helped him break camp and pack the horse and in a few minutes we were headed for the ranch.

I'd thought earlier about trying to go get Old Dobbin, but I wasn't eager to go up against the two gunmen, Slim and Jeb just yet. Old Dobbin would be all right with them and my job now was to get them cattle back before Fink sold them and had them loaded in cattle cars headed for one of them big eastern cities.

It was nigh on to midnight before we reached the R Bar R and everything was dark, which didn't fret me any. Nobody in his right mind would be up at midnight. I unsaddled the horses and turned them loose in the corral while Sears took the pack off the third horse. I went over and banged on the bunkhouse door so as not to startle Blackie and Lew and went on in, with Sears right behind me.

It was quiet in there, too quiet. I fumbled around and found the lantern, fumbled some more and found a match and lit the lantern. I lifted it up to get a better light and looked around the room. There wasn't anybody there.

"Dang," I said, setting the lantern on the table. "I told them boys to stay around here 'til I got back."

"Don't look like they mean to come back," Sears commented. "They ain't nuthin here. They've took their bedrolls and everything else."

He was right. Lew and Blackie had cleared out bag and baggage.

My bedroll was still on my bunk, but that was all. All of a sudden I was scared. If they were gone what about Esme and Mary Lou? I headed for the ranch house on the run. I leaped up them stairs and across the porch and began banging on the front door. Nothing. No sound. Nothing.

I tried the front door. It opened to my push. By this time Sears had joined me and he'd been smart enough to bring the lantern.

"I'm scared," I said. "It don't look like nobody's home and there oughtta be. Somethin' is damn wrong."

I taken the lantern from Sears and we went on in. Everything seemed to be in place in the living room but the house felt empty. I found and lit another lantern and handed it to Sears, then we went on into the kitchen. Everything was in place there, too. No dirty dishes in the sink. Nothing. I felt of the stove. It was cold.

We went into the hallway that led to the bedrooms, and then I thought I heard a scratching noise. I stopped and listened and heard it again. It was coming from Esme's bedroom.

"Beauty?" I said, my voice echoing through the hallway. A whine came through the door. I opened it and Beauty was standing there. She was shaking from thirst and hunger but when I put my hand down she licked it.

"You keep lookin'," I said to Sears. "I got to get Beauty here some water. Looks like she's been penned up a while."

I hurried to the kitchen with Beauty staggering after me, found a bowl and pumped some water into it. I looked around and found some bread and a pan half filled with beans. I tore the bread into little chunks and mixed it in with some of the beans in another bowl and set it on the floor. Beauty went after it like it was a T-bone steak.

About then Jack Sears walked into the kitchen. "Nothin'," he said. "House is all neat and tidy but ain't nobody here."

"Dang it all to hell," I said. "There's somethin' sure wrong here. But there's nothin' we can do 'til daylight. Maybe then we can pick up some sign."

"You don't suppose them rustlers what have been stealin' your cows have taken to stealin' your women, do ya?" Sears asked.

"Don't know," I said. "We'll maybe find out in the mornin'."

The night passed slow. I didn't get much sleep, lying there trying to figure out what had happened to everybody. Folks just don't disappear. There's always a reason. Furthermore, Lew and Blackie hadn't seemed the kind who would cut and run. I finally drifted off sometime in the early hours, but, as usual I was up at daybreak. Beauty, who'd slept on the floor by my bunk, followed me out.

Hunger pangs were gnawing at me so I went on to the kitchen and started a fire. I nosed around and found some coffee which I made first off. In the pantry I found both eggs and bacon as well as some bread. Sears walked in about the time I was putting breakfast on the table. I'd already fed Beauty and she was outside taking care of her morning duties.

Sears poured himself a mugful of coffee and took a swallow. "Taste's good for a change," he said, smacking his lips.

We ate in a hurry and I just piled the dishes in the sink. Wiping his mouth with the back of his sleeve Sears looked at me and said, "Too bad to be losin' a good cook like you."

I ignored him and headed outside to see if I could pick up any kind of sign. First thing I did was check the barn. Baby, Esme's Appaloosa mare, was gone which meant there was a good chance she'd ridden off. We saddled up and began circling the ranch cutting for sign but I was never much of a tracker. Coming out of those California mountains the way I did I could spot a grizzly track and tell one from a brown bear and I knew a cougar track when I saw one, but all horse tracks looked pretty much alike to me. I knew a puncher once down in Texas who could track a snake across a flat rock, but that sure wasn't me.

"You much at trackin'?" I asked Sears.

He shook his head. "That's for Injuns and breeds," he said. "Far as I'm concerned you seen one horse track you seen 'em all."

"You ain't much good for anything but shootin' and fightin', are ya," I said.

"Drinkin'," he answered. "All us Searses are good drinkers."

After an hour I gave up. I'd spotted a hoofprint here and there but I couldn't follow them long enough to give me any idea of where they were going.

"I'm headin' for the Lazy A," I said. "If they ain't there I'm goin' on to town. If they ain't there I'm gonna run down Fink and beat the truth out of him. They got to be somewhere and they've either ridden off or Fink has got 'em.''

"I'll come along,'' Sears said. "I wouldn't want anyone else to get the first shot at ya.''

We taken off at a good clip. From the map Billy Bob had drawn I had a pretty good idea of where the Lazy A was situated. It lay south and east of the R Bar R, over against one of the mountains to the south of Early Mountain but still a ways north of Nora.

We'd been riding more than an hour when we came over a rise and looked over an expanse of green that put the R Bar R grazing land to shame. White-faced cattle were grazing peacefully all the way up to the base of the mountain which was about a mile away. Over against the mountain was a cluster of buildings that I taken to be the Lazy A, which didn't surprise me none since all the cattle I saw were wearing the Lazy A brand.

I turned to Sears. "Chances are nobody at the Lazy A knows either one of us. Let's circle around and come in from the south.''

He didn't argue and we turned and rode back behind the rise and had followed it south for nearly an hour when we came across the trail that led from the road coming north out of Nora to the Lazy A.

"They'll think we've come from Nora,'' I said.

The Lazy A was a good-looking outfit. No matter if Fink was a rustler and a killer, he ran a tight ship. The ranch and outbuildings were in good shape and there wasn't any junk equipment lying around.

There was a tough looking, redheaded puncher sitting on the front porch of the ranch house and a Winchester leaning against the wall beside him. There was another man kind of slouched against the side of what I took to be the bunkhouse. He was wearing two guns.

He was tall and pasty-faced with greasy black hair that hung to his shoulders. I knew him right off. He was Jump Cassidy, an Arizona gunfighter, who never fought for fun, only for money. I'd seen him in action once down near Yuma. He'd killed a man in a fair fight, but from what I'd heard he'd as soon shoot you from behind.

"Howdy," I said to the redhead. "Boss around?"

"Nope," he replied. "But it don't matter. We ain't hiring and we don't need no saddle bums loafin' around, so I'd advise ya to ride on."

"That ain't very neighborly," Sears said. He'd been riding with his rifle across his saddle and now he kind of swung it with his left hand so it was pointing in the redhead's general direction.

"I said to ride on," the redhead said, standing up and glaring at us.

Jump Cassidy had strolled over to about 10 feet from the redhead and I turned my horse so I was facing him.

"You heard what he said," Cassidy said. "Ride on."

He leaned forward to get a better look at me. "Say," he said. "Don't I know you?"

"Could be," I said. "I been around."

The shock of recognition swept across his narrow face. And then he laughed without humor. "Yeah, I know you," he said. "You're Tackett."

"Somebody finally got it right," I said.

"You got a lot of nerve comin' here," he said.

"Just trying to be neighborly." I said.

"In a pig's eye," he said. "You're huntin' trouble and you come to the right place.

"I got this one, Red. You take the cripple."

He went for his guns, but I hadn't waited for him to finish talking. My gun was half out of its holster before he made his move. He saw it and knew he was going to die if he tried to finish drawing. He stopped the downward movement of his hands and thrust them out from his side.

"You win," he said. He wasn't afraid. He wasn't no coward. He just didn't see any point in bucking a stacked deck.

I looked over at Red. He was standing with his hands half raised. Sears was handling that Winchester like a pistol. He was holding it in his left hand with his finger on the trigger and the muzzle aimed dead center on Red's chest.

"So much for being friends," I said. "Now you fellers turn around and very slow and very careful unbuckle yer gun belts and drop 'em on the ground."

If looks could kill they wouldn't have needed their guns, but after a second's hesitation they did as I told them. "The two of you move over against the wall of the house and face it," I ordered.

When they'd done that I swung down from my saddle and went over to them. "Both of you unbuckle yer belts and hand them to me," I ordered.

They grumbled some but the feel of my gun muzzle against the back of his neck persuaded Cassidy to do what I wanted.

"Tell him," I said to Cassidy. "Old Jack Sears there has a itchy trigger finger."

"Do it, Red," he said. "Our turn'll come."

"Put yer hands behind your backs," I ordered a third time.

They did as I said and I wrapped their belts around their wrists pulled them snug and buckled them. "You can turn around now," I said. "And head for the bunkhouse."

I followed behind them on foot and Sears rode, still keeping his rifle trained on them. When we got there I stood them in front of the door while I stood to one side and pushed it open. If someone was waiting inside it wasn't me who was going to be in their sights. But nothing happened.

I shoved them on inside and followed them in. The place was empty except for two men sitting in chairs on opposite sides of the room. It was Lew and Blackie and neither one of them rose to greet me because they were both tied up.

"Howdy, fellers," I said. "Long time no see."

They didn't say anthing, just looked at me. I went over and untied them. They stood gingerly, flexing their legs and chafing their wrists.

"You took long enough," Lew grumbled.

"Where are the girls," I asked.

"Don't know," Lew said. "Probably in the house."

I handed him my gun. "You and Blackie take care of these two. Sears and me'll go look in the house."

By now Sears had climbed down from his horse and we headed for the house. When we got there I picked up one of Jump Cassidy's guns and stuck it in my holster. Then I went up the stairs and across the porch and kicked the door open. It opened into a big living room. There was a Mexican woman sitting by one of the doors leading back into the house. She looked about 25 and was pretty in a sullen and voluptuous way. You could tell, another five years and she'd have gone from voluptuous to fat.

She stood up when we walked in and didn't say anything. But she nodded yes when I asked if she spoke English.

"What's in there," I asked, gesturing at the door.

"Nothing, senor," she said sullenly.

I went over and tried the handle. It was locked.

"Gimme the key," I demanded.

"I no have," she replied.

"We'll see," I said. "I'm gonna search ya."

Sears laughed. "Lemme help," he said.

I reached for her blouse and she shrank back, covering her breasts with crossed hands. "Gimme," I said.

She reached into a pocket of her skirt and pulled out a key.

I taken it and unlocked the door. It was a small, dark, window-less room. Through the gloom I made out a figure on a narrow cot. It sat up when I came in and I saw it was a woman.

"Esme," I said questioningly?

"It's Mary Lou," she said. "I don't know where Esme is."

She swung around, stood up and came toward me.

"I'm glad you found me, Mr. Tackett," she said. "I was afraid nobody would come."

I took her by the hand and led her into the living room. In the light I could see she had been crying. She looked pale and her dress was torn, but otherwise she appeared to be all right.

"He called me a whore," she said brokenly. "And said when they came back he was going to let his men take turns with me."

Sears was standing next to her and she turned blindly to him and began sobbing on his shoulder. With an embarassed look on his face he put his arms around her to comfort her.

I turned to the Mexican woman. "Where's the other woman?"

"I do not know. They took her away."

"Where? Who took her."

"Senor Fink took her I do not know where."

I drew back my fist threateningly. "Yer lyin'."

"It will do you no good to hit me, senor," she said. "I do not know where."

"When are they comin' back?"

"I do not know, senor. Maybe a week, maybe longer."

"You don't know nuthin', do ya," I snarled. I turned to Sears. "Let's go see if we can do better with Cassidy or Red," I rasped.

"I'll tie up the senorita here," he said. "She may have a gun stashed somewhere. Me and the little lady'll be along directly."

I headed for the bunkhouse where I found Lew and Blackie waiting. Red and Jump Cassidy were tied securely to the chairs.

I turned to Cassidy. "Where'd Fink take the other woman?"

He shrugged. "No idea."

"Look," I said. "I ain't got time to fool with you. I'm gonna begin and cut you into little ribbons. And when I through with you I'd gonna start in on Red here. Now talk, dammit."

He just looked at me. I reached down and fetched my knife from the sheath buckled low on my right calf. I placed the point against his cheek and pressed until blood began oozing around it. He looked right at me without flinching. Then he shrugged again.

"Damned if you wouldn't do it. Damned if you wouldn't cut me. I ain't afraid of you, mister, but Fink ain't payin' me enough to take a cuttin'."

"Where is she?" I rasped. I was beginning to feel an uncontrollable anger building up in me.

"Ain't sure," he said. "He said something about Nora or Nora's. It's a town or a place or somethin' I wouldn't know. I came down here from Denver a couple of weeks ago and I ain't never been in this part of the country before."

I turned to Red and showed him the point of my knife. "I wouldn't mind workin' on you."

He'd already turned pale and now he turned snow white. "Won't do ya no good," he said. "I was out on the range when they raided yer ranch and I didn't know 'til now that there was another woman."

"He's tellin' the truth," Cassidy said.

Just then Sears came into the bunkhouse pushing the Mexican woman in front of him. "Thought these boys might like some company," he said. "We kin tie her to one of the bunks."

She started to protest. "Lady, I'll slug you if I have to. It won't bother me none," Sears said.

He turned to me, gesturing with his bad hand. "You better do it," he said. "Tie her tight."

In a few minutes she was tied to the bunk.

"Adios, senors and senorita," I said, as we turned to go.

"Wait a minute," Red said. "What are we gonna do for water and food?"

"You shoulda thought about that afore you joined up with Fink," I said.

I paused a moment. "Tell ya what. After we find Esme we'll come back and feed ya. You better pray we find her quick."

I went outside where the others were waiting. "I'm goin' in to Nora," I said. "It's likely that Esme's there somewhere."

"I'll go with you," Lew said.

"There may be some shootin'," I said.

"Let's go," he said.

"Jack," I said to Sears. "Best thing for you uns to do is go on back to the R Bar. If we ain't back in a couple of days, might be a good idea to clear out. The three of you ain't no match for Fink and his gang."

"You go along," Sears said. "You don't come back we'll figure somethin'."

By this time Lew had found his saddle where it had been left in the barn. In a couple of minutes he'd roped one of the horses in the corral and was ready to go. I climbed aboard the big roan I'd taken from the rustler in the hidden valley and we taken off at a fast trot for Nora.

CHAPTER 9

As WE TROTTED off toward Nora I heard Jack Sears hollering after us, "Don't you run out on me, Tackett. I'll be waitin' fer ya."

I grinned in spite of myself. Sears was still bent on killing me, or at least trying to make me think he was. I sure didn't want to kill him; he'd saved my life. And after what we'd been through together, I couldn't think he was still serious. But still, when I came back—if I came back—we were going to have to have it out once and for all, if that's really what he wanted.

I finally thought to ask Lew what had happened back at the R Bar R and it was simple. Half a dozen men, including Fink, had ridden up to the ranch before dawn the morning after I left and burst into the bunkhouse while Lew and Blackie were sleeping. After they took them prisoner they went to the main house and rousted the women out of bed.

"They caught us plumb by surprise. Wasn't a dang thing we could do," Lew said.

After that we were silent on the rest of the ride into Nora. Neither one of us was the talkative type and, besides, I had some thinking to do.

Where had they taken Esme? And why had they taken her? Nora wasn't much of a town, if they'd taken her there. I could tear it apart in less than a day and I was going to if I had to. But suppose she wasn't there? Had Fink taken her with him on the cattle drive to Chambers? Had he stashed her at one of those rawhide ranches over against Mountains? I had no answers, just questions, but I was sure of one thing. If she wasn't in Nora I was going to ride to Chambers and wait for Fink there and when I got to him I was going to beat the information out of him. And then maybe, just maybe, I was going to kill him.

The thought that something might have happened to Esme made me shrivel up inside. She was pretty, she was sweet and caring, she was smart and competent and brave. There on that ride it occurred to me, not suddenly, but gradual-like. I was in love with her.

Damn! That was the last thing I wanted and the last thing I figured that she would want. I was just a drifting saddle tramp. I had no money, no family, no education. All I had was my gun and my saddle and Old Dobbin and I wasn't sure about Old Dobbin at the moment. I was going to have to get him back from the Fink gang.

She, on the other hand, was pretty much the aristocrat. She came from a fine family. She was well educated. And if I could save her ranch for her she would be, if not rich, at least well off.

I was determined to save her ranch even if it meant continuing to risk my life. Once that was done I'd ride out. There was a lot of the world left to see and a lot of pretty girls, too. And I'd go looking.

By the time I'd finished this line of reasoning, if you could call it that, we were almost to Nora. We pulled the horses up and talked a minute.

"Look," I said. "I don't know what's going to happen in there. I just gotta start lookin' and it may be that she's not here. What I need for you to do is watch my back. I don't know all the players in this game and I don't wanna get caught by surprise."

Lew nodded. "Whatever you say," he said. "I'll play it yer way."

Ten minutes later we were riding down Nora's one dusty, rutty street. There was only a dozen or so buildings along it, including the two saloons, and a scattering of houses on the far end and around the edges. And there at the end of the street was that big, two-story adobe, shaded by tall cottonwoods, that housed Nora and her girls.

We pulled up in front of the general store and dismounted. The sign on the unpainted, clapboard building said, "Weed's Emporium." It was rumored the owner had named it after his home town, Emporium, Kansas. There was an old man behind the counter. I judged him to be about fifty. He was white haired and pink cheeked and he looked like he'd been eating as many of his groceries as he sold. His name was Ludlow Weed. I knew who he was because when I'd first come to town I'd had occasion to buy some ammunition from him.

He looked at me with little pig eyes that were doubly wreathed in fat and steel-rimmed spectacles.

"Howdy, Mr. Weed," I said.

"I know you?" he asked.

"Been in here once," I said. "A while back. Bought some shells."

"Yeah," he said. "I remember. What can I do for you."

"I been ramroddin' the R Bar R, the Rankin outfit. And I was supposed to meet Miss Rankin here in Nora. You seen her?"

"She hasn't been in here today," he said. "Or for that matter for four or five weeks. Have you tried the cafe down the street?"

I looked him in the eye and saw greed but no guile. "I'll try it," I said.

"If you see her tell her that cloth material she asked me to order has come in. She'll know what I'm talking about."

"I'll tell her," I said, walking out the door, with Lew trailing behind.

Weed had built a boardwalk in front of the Emporium but after that you walked in the dirt alongside the street to get where you were going.

To get to the cafe, which you could tell because the sign over the door said "EATS," we had to pass the stage station and an empty building whose sign said "JAIL," but that was a laugh because the nearest law was in Chambers, fifty miles to the south.

I stuck my head in the stage office. There was a nondescript young fellow leaning on the counter reading a month-old newspaper.

"Any stages left here in the last day or two?" I asked.

"Nope," he said, without looking up. "But one's due in tomorrow."

I thanked him and and went on to the jail. I tried the door and it was unlocked. Inside was a room with a single cell built into the corner. It wasn't meant to hold anyone very long. It didn't hold anybody at all now. Across the room was a busted chair and a dusty desk. That was all. I closed the door and went on to the "EATS" cafe.

It was like most of the other buildings in town, clapboard, unpainted, and weatherbeaten and warped from the sun and rain and wind. Lew and I pushed our way in. There was one long table down one side of the room and three small tables along the other wall. There was a cowhand putting away some beans and beef at the big table. He gave us an indifferent glance and kept on eating.

At one of the small tables there were two of the town women drinking tea and chatting, just like they were in a big city. Neither one was was very old, but both were weatherworn and careworn. Both were also dolled up in their finest, which wasn't very fine, and doing their dangdest to pretend that things were better than they were. I felt sorry for them and envied them at the same time.

There was a waitress hovering around the back of the room, scrawny, mouse-colored hair, mouse-colored dress, mousy. It taken me just a few seconds to take this all in, then I shifted my gaze back to the cowboy. I knew I'd seen him somewhere before.

Bingo! I said to myself. I turned to Lew. "Get them ladies outta here. Quick!" I whispered. "There may be some shootin'."

The cowboy eating at the big table was the rustler who'd been with Evan Stevens in the cabin in the hidden valley.

I eased my gun out and held it alongside my leg. At the same time I moved around to the other side of the long table and sat down across from the puncher.

He still hadn't looked up. "Friend," I said, easylike. "Keep on eatin' but just remember there's a gun pointed at you under the table."

Now he looked up, a puzzled expression on his face. Then he half came out of his seat in surprise.

"Easy does it. There's a gun pointin' at ya under the table," I reminded him.

He wasn't no fool. He sank down on his chair and put both hands flat on the table. His face was white.

"I didn't have nothin' to do with them wantin' to kill ya," he said.

"I s'pose you didn't have nothin' to do with rustlin' R Bar cows, neither," I said.

"I quit," he said shakily. "I done quit 'em. I didn't know them was rustled cows."

"Yer a liar," I said, raising my gun above the table so he could see it was pointed right at him.

By this time Lew had hustled the two women out of there and was standing over by the mousy waitress who was looking slack-jawed at my gun.

"All's clear, boss," he said. "Go ahead and have yer fun."

The cowboy went to pick up his coffee but his hand was trembling so much he had to set it down.

"I know you," he said. "Yer one of them Sackett gunslingers from up around Mora. Yer gonna kill me, ain't ya?"

"Them Sacketts must be mean fellers," I said.

"You oughtta know. Yer one," he whispered hoarsely.

"If I shoot ya you'll be dead and it won't matter none what my name is," I said. "And right now I don't give a damn about cows. What I want to know and what yer gonna tell me is where Esme Rankin is."

"I don't know no Esme Rankin," he said.

I stood up and leaned over and backhanded him across the face. "Keep lyin'," I said, "and you'll be beggin' me to shoot ya."

My knuckles scraping across his face had bloodied his lips. He wiped them off with the back of his sleeve. "I don't know," he whispered again.

I slapped him again, harder, and his chair went over backwards and he sprawled on the floor. I went over the table after him and landed with my knee in his belly. All the air went out of him with a whoof, his face went from white to green and he rolled over on his side and threw up.

When he'd finished I yanked him to his feet by the front of his shirt and holding him up I slapped him back and forth across the face half a dozen times.

"Don't," he whimpered finally. "No more."

"Where is she, you lousy sonofabitch?" I snarled. I was so worked up I never even thought about Ma not liking that kind of talk.

He spit out some blood. "Nora's," he said.

I turned to the waitress who was watching wide-eyed. "Clean this place up," I said. "And remember, you ain't seen nothin' and you don't know nothin'."

"Yes, sir," she squeaked.

All of a sudden there was a noise behind me. When I looked I saw Lew, gun in hand, standing over the cowboy who was sprawled on the floor again.

"What did ya do that for?" I asked.

"You forgot to get his gun. He was reachin' for it," he said laconically.

I shook my head. Another careless mistake. I wasn't going to live very long if I kept this up.

The cowboy groaned and struggled to a sitting position. Lew reached down and hauled him to his feet again. He'd kicked the cowboy's gun over against the wall and now he went over and picked it up and stuffed it behind his belt.

"What're we gonna do with this hombre?" he asked. "Kill him?"

"Not yet," I said. "Let's take him to the jail and see if we can find a key."

The street was empty when we went outside and we hustled the cowboy the few yards to the jail. Inside I rummaged through the paper-littered desk drawer and to my surprise found a key. It fit the cell door, so we shoved the cowboy into the cell and locked it behind him.

"Pray that we come back," I told him. "Otherwise you might be in here a long time."

We walked back to the Emporium and climbed aboard our horses. Ludlow Weed had seen us and came to the door. "Find her?" he asked.

"No," I said. "If she comes by, tell her to wait here. I'll be back later."

"Wife says there was trouble at the cafe."

"Little scuffle, that's all. Everything's fine."

Before he could ask any more questions I wheeled the roan and we headed off for Nora's. I took my hat off and scratched my head. Dang, what would Esme be doing there? Why would Fink take her to Nora's? It didn't make no sense that the town madam would be in cahoots with Fink. Or did it? Come to think of it I didn't know hardly anything about either one of them. I knew Nora had been the town's first settler and that she'd come into this country about ten years back and built that big adobe house. Even at fifty or so she was a good-looking figure of a woman, but that didn't tell me much.

She had a reputation for treating her girls right and she didn't take no nonsense from her clients. She'd seemed glad when I'd run Evan Stevens out of there that day. And she'd been willing for me to take Mary Lou out of there. But still, none this told me why she might be holding Esme.

I knew even less about Fink. He'd come into the territory about two years ago posing as an honest rancher. Now it was plain he was no such thing. Not only had he stolen R Bar R cattle and was planning to sell them, but he also was mixed up in murders, attempted murders, and kidnapping. He or one of his men had killed Billy Bob Doyle and twice they'd try to kill me. And they'd kidnapped Esme and Mary Lou along with Lew and Blackie.

But where he'd come from or what his background was or who he really was I had no idea. He looked familiar but that didn't mean nothing. I'd been wandering for over twelve years and had run into a lot of people during that time.

We rode up to Nora's and tied our horses to her hitching rail and went up and knocked on the heavy front door. The Mexican woman who I'd seen there before opened it and invited us in, probably thinking we were paying customers, which come to think of it, at another time we might have been.

We handed her our hats and went on into the big sitting room. Nora was not there. Instead, a blond woman, somewhere in her thirties and handsome in a hard way, greeted us. She was dressed for walking out, not for staying in. Two other women, one a blond and the other with brown hair, both much younger and dressed for the profession they had chosen, were talking over in a corner. They started to get up when they saw us but I waved them off.

"Nora around?" I asked the older woman.

"She's not available at the moment. May I help you?" she said in a cultured voice.

"Need to talk to Nora," I said.

"I'm sorry but as I said she's not available at the moment."

I lost my patience. "Make her available," I growled.

She drew herself up, not at all afraid. "Sir, if you've come for pleasure we can help you. If you've come to see Nora we can't help you and I will have to ask you to leave."

"Don't get uppity with me, lady," I snarled. "Either you bring Nora out here or I'll start lookin' for her."

She sighed. "Very well, then. Wait here, please."

As she turned away I saw her hand move up to her bosom. On impulse I took one long stride, reached around her and grabbed her wrist. She gasped in surprise and I heard something go clunk on the floor. I looked and saw that it was a little two-barrel derringer.

I swung her around facing me.

"Now why would you want to do somethin' like that?" I asked, still holding on to her wrist.

She struggled to free it, so I let go. But she didn't move back. Instead she stood right up close and glared at me.

"Because you're a goddam bully and I hate bullies," she spat. "You damn men, you always think you can push women around."

I was the one who stepped back. She'd got me right where it hurt. Ma had always taught me to be considerate of women folk and here I was pushing this blond woman around. I knew what she was, but she was also a woman and I knew Ma wouldn't approve. "Lady," I said in a softer voice, "I don't mean to be no bully. But there's somethin' goin' on here and I'm gonna find out about it one way or another. I don't wanna hurt you or no one, but I will if I have to. Now, let's you and me go find Nora."

I taken her by the elbow and started for the stairway, but just then one of the downstairs doors opened and Nora came in, looking cool and dignified, with every hair in place. She was wearing a fancy silk dress that I knew she hadn't bought—couldn't buy—at Lud Weed's Emporium.

"What seems to be the trouble here?" she asked. "Is there something I can do for you gentlemen?"

"Oh," she said, looking at me. "It's you. Tell me, how is Mary Lou getting along?"

"Where's Esmeralda Rankin?" I demanded bluntly.

She eyed me almost disdainfully. "I don't know what you're talking about, young man."

"I think ya do," I said. "And if you don't bring her out I'm going to tear this place apart."

"Mr. Tackett," she warned. "If you harm me or my place the cowboys from fifty miles around will gather here and in all likelihood lynch you to one of my cottonwood trees."

I laughed without humor. "They find you've harmed one hair on Esme's head and they'll hang you right alongside of me. Now I'm tired of foolin' around. Take me to her."

I'll give it to her, all right. She was a cool one. "What makes you think she's here?" she asked.

"I done had a talk with Jump Cassidy," I said. "He didn't want me to cut on him so he talked."

She never blinked. "Jump Cassidy lied to you."

"Fine," I said. "Then you won't mind if me and Lew take a look around."

"You can't do that," she said. "I have clients upstairs."

"We'll knock first," I said. "That'll give 'em a chance to put their pants on."

Lew spoke up. "Didn't see no horses out in front, ma'am."

That gave me an idea. "Go check the barn, Lew. See if Baby's in there."

"Stay away from that barn, cowboy." Nora spoke sharply.

"Go look, Lew," I said. He didn't answer, just hurried on out the door.

Nora looked at the blond, then over at the two girls who were sitting quietly in the corner. "You girls go to your rooms. Irene, come with me. I've had enough of this nonsense."

"I'd sure hate to have to shoot a woman," I said, drawing my gun. "But I will if you don't sit down."

"You don't frighten me, cowboy," she sneered.

I pulled the trigger on the gun which went off with a loud bang that sounded louder in a closed room. A vase on a table right behind her crashed to the floor in pieces.

"Now sit," I said. She and the blond Irene sat. Nora eyed me thoughtfully.

"People keep saying you're a Sackett," she said. "But you're a Tackett, all right. I never knew a Sackett to be as mean as you are."

"I ain't mean," I said. "I'm just plumb out of patience. You fetch me Esme Rankin and I'll go and leave ya alone. I ain't lookin' for trouble but I ain't walkin' away from it, either."

Just then Lew burst through the door. "Baby's out there," he said.

Nora stared straight ahead and Irene gazed out the window like she was looking for the three wise men.

"I thought you said Jump Cassidy was lyin?" I said.

She turned and looked at me. "I told him not to leave her here," she said. "I'm trying to run an honest business and that fool may have ruined everything."

"Who," I asked. "What fool? Not Jump Cassidy?"

"My son," she said bitterly. "My only son. Reginald P. Fink."

She reached for the silver bell on the table by her side. The Mexican woman came in answer to her ring. Nora reached in her bosom and drew out a key hanging from a gold chain she wore around her neck. She unfastened the chain, removed the key and handed it to the Mexican woman.

"Go bring the lady out who's in the back bedroom, Manuela," she said. "Let her straighten herself up first."

"If you've hurt her I'll . . . "

"Of course not," she interrupted. "They treated her a little roughly on the way here, but she's all right. Reggie wouldn't hurt her. After all, she's his half sister."

CHAPTER 10

I SAT THERE stunned, wondering if I'd heard right, yet knowing that I had.

Esme and Reggie Fink were brother and sister, or at least half brother and sister. And Nora was Fink's mother. That must mean that old Colonel Rankin was their father. If that was so then why wasn't Fink's last name Rankin? It was all pretty confusing to my still aching head.

Lew looked at me inquiringly, wondering what I wanted done. I shook my head. Nothing, for now. Nora sat there with a half-defiant look on her face. The blond, Irene, continued to gaze out the window. Finally the door opened and Esme came into the room.

Her hair needed brushing and her clothes looked like she'd slept in them but otherwise she appeared to be all right.

Her eyes widened in surprise when she saw me.

"Del!" she exclaimed. I stood up and she flew into my arms. "Oh, thank God! Thank God it's you."

She started to cry and I held her close, stroking the back of her head. After a minute she calmed down and looked up at me.

"I thought you were dead," she said brokenly. "They were going to do terrible things to me."

She looked at Irene and shrank back, pointing a finger at her.

"It's awful," she said. "That terrible woman. She came into the room and said she was going to wait until Nora was gone, then she was going to make l-l-love to me."

She started to cry again. I looked at Nora. She shrugged.

"To each her own," she said. Then when she saw my look of disgust, she added, "Men can be so cruel."

She turned to Irene who continued to look out the window. "We'll talk later," she said coldly.

"They tell you about your—about Reggie?" I asked.

"He told me he's my brother—my half brother, but I don't believe him."

"It's true," Nora said.

"He can't be. He's mean and vicious. He hit me. He said he was going to take me to Mexico and turn me into a-a-a." She stopped and then wailed, "Ohhh, I can't say it," and buried her head on my chest.

I looked at Nora again. "What kind of people are you?" I said.

"Reggie hates her," she said. "I taught him to hate her and to hate her father—his father."

I never said anything but the question, Why? was plain on my face.

"He seduced me when I was only fifteen and he was twenty," she said in a voice devoid of emotion. "He was a cadet at West Point who had come home on leave. When I found I was pregnant I wrote him and he wrote back that he would marry me after he graduated. But he didn't. I never heard from him again. Instead he went off and left me with a baby in my belly and no money. I had shamed my parents and they sent me away. They said nice girls didn't sleep with men. They never blame the man; they always blame the woman. I almost starved until after the baby—Reggie—was born.

"Afterward I made a living the only way I could—with my body. I was pretty then. And I was good. No man ever went away disappointed. Some of them paid me a lot of money, but none of them wanted a mistress who had a baby, or wife who was a whore.

"After a few years I had saved enough money to come west, to Santa Fe. I thought I would start over, but there's no decent work for a woman who has no education, no training. So I went back to doing the one thing I knew, but I was fussy about my clients. No unwashed, stinking cowboys for me.

"I made enough money to send Reggie to school in the east. He never knew until later where it came from.

"One day on a street in Santa Fe, I saw this handsome couple, an army officer and a beautiful Spanish-looking lady. They had a child with them—a girl about three or four. I knew him in an instant—he was John Rankin, my onetime lover and the father of my son.

"I thought to accost him there on the street, but I knew it wouldn't do any good. Who would believe a woman in my business? But I followed them home and over the years I watched them. He would be sent to some other station but she always remained in Santa Fe with her."

She nodded at Esme.

"Go on," I said.

"When Reggie came home the summer he was eighteen, I sat him down and told him the facts of life. Who I was, who he was, who his father was, where the money came from. It almost killed him. I can hear him now, screaming, 'My mother's a whore.' He rushed out of the house and I never saw him again for nearly eight years.

"When he came home I hardly recognized him. He wasn't the eastern gentleman I'd wanted to make him into. He was wearing a beard—and a gun. His hair was long and he was dressed like a cowboy. But he wasn't a cowboy; he was a gunslinger. He told me he had killed seven men including three in a cattle war over near the Texas border. He said he hired his gun out instead of his body.

"He said he'd changed his name to Ray Failor."

I interrupted her. "Ray Failor? I thought I knew him. He's a fast man with a gun. I thought he's been killed over in east Texas. I guess I was wrong."

She nodded. "You were," she said. "He planted that rumor after he came home. It was part of our plan.

"When he came home he told me that he'd had time to do a lot of thinking and that he realized that what I'd done I'd done for him. He said he forgave me and would I forgive him. Of course I did. He told me he'd sworn to get even with his father, kill him, if it came to that. He said he could never take his father's name, but he'd take everything else he had including his daughter.

"We hated her, both of us. She had everything we should have had. His name, his money, a position in society when she grew up.

"My family name was Fink and that's the name he used all the time he was growing up. He thought that was my married name, that I was a widow. I'd used the name Wetstone professionally to keep him from being embarassed. I took it from a fine old man who died in my arms one night back east.

"That was quite a night. Another girl and I had to dress him and get him out of the house and across town where they found him the next day. When we got home we discovered we'd forgotten to put his underwear on. I've often wondered what the police thought.

"After Reggie came home he cut his hair and shaved his beard and went to work in the bank there in Santa Fe. And he was good. He worked there for over five years and when he quit he'd stolen nearly ten thousand dollars from them and they never knew it."

She said it proudly, and went on while Esme and Lew and me listened in fascination.

"Most nights he gambled and he was good at that, too, so by the time he quit the bank he had more than enough money to buy that ranch.

"It wasn't long after Reggie came home that his father's—he was a colonel by now—his father's wife died. It was pneumonia, I think. After that the colonel disappeared. We inquired around discreetly and found he'd retired and moved up here to start ranching. He sent his daughter to school back east where he had kin while he was building the ranch.

"As soon as I found he'd come up here, I took all my savings— by now I was running my own place and letting younger girls do the work—and came up here and built this place. It was a good move. There were a lot of ranches around and no girls except a few Indians and Mexicans.

"I was the first one here and they've even built a town around me," she said with satisfaction.

She continued: "When the owner of the Lazy A wanted to sell, I sent for Reggie and he bought the place. After that we plotted how to bankrupt the colonel and send him and her," she nodded at Esme, "to the poorhouse.

"We never thought he'd fall off his horse and kill himelf. But it didn't matter that much. By now Reggie had found that hidden valley and was using it to hide R Bar R cows in. And he was running off her hired hands. And all was going just fine and he was going to be the biggest rancher in this part of Arizona and then you came along.

"He should have killed you when he had the chance," she added bitterly. "He knows it, too."

"If you see him first tell him not to worry. He'll get his chance," I said.

I looked at Esme and Lew.

"This place stinks," I said. "Let's get out of here."

I taken Esme by the hand and, with Lew trailing, we headed for the door. We left those two bitter women sitting there and went out into the sunshine. Esme and I waited while Lew went around to the barn and saddled Baby and brought her around.

"This thing is about wound up," I told Esme while we were waiting. "But I got to ride to Chambers. Fink is drivin' your cattle there and he's got a buyer waitin'. I want that you should go back to the ranch with Lew. Mary Lou and Blackie and Jack Sears are there and you'll be safe 'til I get back."

"I'm going with you," she said. "They're my cattle."

"You can't go like that," I said, pointing to her dress.

"We can go over to the Emporium and Mr. Weed can sell me some clothes. I know his wife will let me change at their house."

"There's likely to be shootin'," I said.

"They're my cattle," she repeated. "And I'm going with you."

Before I could argue further Lew came around with Baby who was wearing a sidesaddle.

Esme climbed on her, and I said, "If you're even thinkin' of comin' with me we have to get you jeans and a real saddle."

"Mr. Weed sells saddles," she said.

"Lew," I said. "We're going over to the Emporium and outfit Esme so she can come with us to Chambers. You take the key and go turn that feller loose we put in the jail."

He headed for the jail and we trotted over to the Emporium, which was still open even though the sun was beginning to go down. Lud Weed's eyebrows went up when he saw Esme and noticed the shape of her hair and clothes, but he didn't say nothing. Esme told him what she needed and then asked if it would be all right with his wife if she changed at their home.

"No problem, Miss Esmeralda," he said. "Mrs. Weed will be delighted to see you. Perhaps you and Mr. Tackett could stay for dinner."

"Looks like you eat well at your house," I said.

"We do," he said with a chuckle that set his massive belly to quivering.

Just then Lew came hurrying in.

"He's gone," he said. "Busted out. Them bars was just set in wood at the top and he worked 'em lose enough to spring the lock. No wonder they don't use the damn jail. Wouldn't be no good for anything but drunks."

"Lew," I said. "You got to get out to the ranch and warn 'em. I'll bet two-bits that feller is headed for the Lazy A. If I'm right he'll turn Jump Cassidy and Red loose and they'll head for the R Bar and see if they can catch Blackie and Jack asleep. Get goin'."

When he'd left I said to Weed, "It's late and we got a long ways to go tomorrow. I'd like to arrange for Miss Esmeralda to stay at your house tonight so we can get an early start in the morning."

"I think we can arrange that," he said. "Soon as I lock up we'll go over to the house for dinner and I'll see what Mrs. Weed can arrange."

The Weed house was only about fifty yards in back of the store and while Esme and Weed walked to it I taken the horses to his small barn, unsaddled them, and rubbed the big roan down. It was a four-stall barn and Weed kept only one horse and that left one for me to sleep in.

I stopped outside at the well pump and filled a handy tin pan with water and rinsed off my face and hands and went on up to the house.

Mrs. Weed was one of the ladies I'd had Lew hustle out of the cafe earlier in the day and she thanked me for that.

I'd noticed some chickens out in a coop but there was one less than there'd been the day before, and it was on the table, along with potatoes and gravy and some greens she'd grown in her backyard garden. She had a dried peach pie for dessert and after watching Lud Weed eat I could see why he wasn't any thinner. After we'd eaten she poured some coffee. It was hot and black and strong, and it tasted good. And I told her so.

When I'd finished I got up from my chair and said good night.

"If you don't mind I'll be sleepin' in the empty stall in the barn," I said. "I'd appreciate it if you could rouse Miss Esme early. We got a long way to go."

During dinner I'd explained that we had to get to Chambers but I didn't tell them why and even though I knew they were busting with curiosity they didn't ask.

There was enough hay to make a comfortable mattress for my bedroll and I went right off to sleep. It had been a long, hard day and I still wasn't a hundred percent well and sleep was what I needed most. Even so I awoke as usual at first light.

By the time I'd pulled on my pants and boots, rolled my bedroll and splashed some water on my face there were signs of activity in the house. I picked up an armload of kindling and knocked on the kitchen door. Mrs. Weed let me in and rewarded me for the load of wood with a cup of coffee. She was a matronly woman with gray hair and beginning to thicken in the waist. But she was like her kitchen, warm and hospitable, and she had a face that twenty years ago would have been called pretty.

By the time I'd finished my coffee, Mrs. Weed was putting

breakfast on the table. Lud Weed came in and sat down followed a moment later by Esme. She looked a sight better than when I'd left her the night before. Her black hair was done up in a bun in preparation for the long trip ahead, but it was a clean, shiny black with just that hint of red in it and it was clear she'd found the time to wash it. Her face was scrubbed clean and the man's shirt and jeans she was wearing didn't do much to hide her figure.

In spite of what she'd just been through and what we were going into she was smiling and gave us a cheery good morning. We ate in hurry and while Esme was finishing her coffee and thanking the Weeds I went out and saddled the horses. After she mounted up it taken me just a minute to adjust her stirrups and then we were waving good bye and heading for Chambers, fifty miles away.

It was a warm late spring day, but a breeze coming down off the mountains kept it from being hot. The stagecoach road was out from the mountains a mite which gave us a view for miles ahead. By noon we'd gone pretty close to twenty miles so when we came across a narrow stream bubbling down from the mountains I turned off and paralleled it until we found a small patch of grass shaded by some good-sized red oaks.

I watered the horses while Esme unwrapped the sandwiches Mrs. Weed had sent along. Esme was still beat from her ordeal of the last few days so I figured to give us an hour to rest up. I asked her if she wanted a nap, but she didn't; she wanted to talk.

"I can't believe that terrible man is my half brother," she said. "He's an evil man. He said that when he came back from selling my cattle he was going to make me deed the R Bar R over to him. He said if I didn't do it he was going to take me to Mexico and turn me over to a woman he knows there, a woman like Nora, only worse. He said she would put me to work."

She shuddered at the thought. "My own brother," she said. "I just can't believe it.

"He told me that even before he came into this country he sent that other awful man, Evan Stevens, up here to get a job with father. He was supposed to gain father's confidence and mine and then marry me. Instead, he killed Father. I still don't believe it. But Reggie said he sneaked up behind Father and hit him on the head. Then he made it look like Father had been thrown from his horse and hit his head on a boulder. Poor Father!

"Reggie said he had a deal with Stevens that if he married me he'd make me sell the ranch to Reggie and then he would keep some of the money and take me away. I don't know where.

"Did you notice that Stevens didn't look or act like a typical cowboy? Well, he wasn't. He'd been to school in the east with Reggie and had ridden with him for four or five years.

"But he wasn't as smart as Reggie and Reggie used him. Reggie said Stevens was good with a gun but not as good as he is."

"Aren't many men around as fast as your brother," I commented.

She went on. "When you killed Stevens, Reggie had to change his plans in a hurry. That's when they decided to kidnap Mary Lou and me. He talked about doing terrible things with Mary Lou and I think he was planning to kill Lew and Blackie and bury them where no one would find them.

"Oh, I'm so glad they didn't kill you. We need you? Beauty and I both need you. Did you notice how she took to you. She never did that with anyone else."

That kind of talk made me uncomfortable. "You better get a bit of a rest," I said. "I'll go check on the horses."

When I came back she was fast asleep. I let her sleep for another half hour, then, after she'd splashed water from the stream on her face, we mounted up and again hit the road for Chambers.

It was midafternoon when I saw signs of a herd of cattle coming into the main trail. We backtracked them for a ways and it turned out that Fink had done what I earlier had figured he would do. He drove the R Bar cattle out the north end of the hidden valley and down around in back of Early Mountain where a narrow valley ran more than halfway to Chambers. That allowed him to drive cattle to Chambers while bypassing Nora and the ranches in the area.

Once he hit the main trail it was a straight shot to Chambers and the railroad.

Up in the valley that day I'd heard Fink tell Stevens that he had a buyer waiting in Chambers. I'd hoped to be waiting there, too, but now it looked like we'd be a little late.

The sun was low and our tired horses had slowed to a walk and Esme was sagging in the saddle when I spotted a dust cloud ahead. It had to be the stolen herd. I figured it was maybe five miles from Chambers.

"I'm gonna leave you here and ride on into Chambers and see if I can spot Fink or find the cattle buyer," I said. "We'll find you a place to wait and I'll come back for ya soon's I find out what's goin' on."

"I'm going with you," she said stubbornly. "I'm tired but I'm all right and I'm not going to let you leave me out here alone."

The horses seemed to sense that the long day was about over. They perked up noticeably and we circled wide around the herd at an easy lope. In an hour we had crossed a wood bridge that spanned the Rio Puerco River and were riding down the main street of Chambers.

It was a bigger town than Nora which it should have been since it was built alongside a spur railroad that also crossed the Rio Puerco. The spur stopped at loading pens that allowed the ranchers north of Chambers to load their cattle without having to drive them across the river.

It was getting dark now, but I spotted the Cattlemen's Hotel about halfway down the main street. We dismounted and went inside where the clerk offered to put us in a room with a double bed. Esme blushed and I told him we weren't married and that the lady would like a room to herself.

The pale young man behind the counter mumbled his apologies and gave us adjacent rooms. I took Esme upstairs to her room and told her she could rest for half an hour and then we'd get some supper. I waited until I heard her lock the door, then I went downstairs and accosted the clerk.

"If I was lookin' for a cattle buyer where would I find him?"

"This time of night, a couple of places," he said. "The Blue Bull saloon which is across the street and down a ways or the Chambers Restaurant which is the fanciest one in town. It's two doors from here in the other direction."

"Any cattle buyers in town that you know of?"

He shook his head. "Sorry, mister. I wouldn't know a cattle buyer if I saw one."

"Neither would I," I said. I thanked him and he went back to his reading.

I figured to try the saloon first. Saloons in western towns are more than just a place to buy a drink, or play cards or talk to a floozie. They're meeting places, places to hear news, and gossip and rumors. You hang around a popular saloon long enough and you'll know who's in town and what's going on.

The Blue Bull was fairly crowded. Men standing at the bar and seated at tables. Some playing cards, some just drinking. I edged up to the bar and ordered a whiskey. I took a sip and it wasn't bad for cow-town rotgut. When I saw that the bartender wasn't busy I signaled him over.

"Any cattle buyers in town that you know of?"

"You with that herd north of town?" he asked.

"In a way," I said. "But right now I'm lookin' for a buyer. You know one?"

"Feller named Andersen, Morton Andersen, was in here last night. Ain't seen him tonight."

I put a silver dollar on the bar. "He comes in, you point him out, huh?"

He slipped the dollar in his pocket and moved away to fill an empty glass. I sipped at mine, watching the crowd in the big mirror behind the bar. Pretty soon the bartender came over.

"Andersen and a feller I don't know just come in," he said. "Andersen's the little guy with the short hair and brown beard."

I turned slowly. Andersen and his companion were making their way toward the other end of the bar. They hadn't seen me.

I set my glass down and edged toward them. They were deep in conversation, paying no attention to folks around them, when I sidled up alongside Andersen.

"Yer dealin' with a thief, Andersen," I said softly.

He whirled around and stared at me. His friend, a handsome man with white teeth and wavy hair, looked up. "Damn you. I should have killed you when I had the chance."

"Ain't too late to try, Fink" I said.

"What's this all about?" Andersen demanded.

"Mr. Andersen, this man is tryin' to sell you five hundred head of cattle that don't belong to him."

He looked at me coldly. "Can you prove that?"

"The owner, Miss Esmeralda Rankin, is across the street."

"I know who she is," he said. "Mr. Fink here has a letter authorizing him to act as her agent in the sale of the cattle."

"I don't know nothin' about that," I said, surprised. "But she's the rightful owner. This here is Ray Failor, the Texas gunman."

"You're wrong, mister. Ray Failor was killed in East Texas several years ago," Andersen said.

"Mr. Andersen, have you bought them cattle yet?" I asked.

"I don't think that's any of your business, young man," he replied.

"Look," I said. "Before you buy 'em, why not talk to Miss Rankin. She can meet you in the lobby of the Cattlemen's Hotel in half an hour."

He pulled out a big pocketwatch and looked at it. "All right," he said grudgingly, "I'll meet you there at eight o'clock but you had better have some proof of ownership because I have cars coming in in the morning and I expect to ship tomorrow."

All this time Fink had been silent. Now I looked at him. "After I've got this straightened out, Fink, me and you got a score to settle."

He smiled mirthlessly. "After we have this straightened out, Tackett, I'm going to kill you."

"Sackett?" Andersen said, looking at me intently. "Are you from up around Mora?"

Fink spoke up before I could answer. "Tackett," he said, "not Sackett. He's a poor imitation of Nolan or Tell or any of them Sacketts I know of."

I ignored him. I wasn't trying to be a Sackett. I just wanted to save the ranch for Esme. And I knew that meant running Fink out of the country or killing him, if it came to that.

"Eight o'clock at the Chambers Cafe," I said to Andersen and started to leave.

Fink said, "Tackett" like he wanted something. He did—my scalp. As I half turned to respond he slugged me in the jaw. He'd caught me off guard with my hands down and I went stumbling backward half a dozen steps and landed on the seat of my pants on the sawdust-covered floor. He followed right after me, and as I was struggling to my feet still half-dazed he hit me again. But this time I'd seen it coming and I managed to duck my head and take the blow on my forehead. I went down again but mostly because I was off balance. He came after me again, this time with his boots, but I managed to roll to one side and scramble to my feet.

I was mad clear through and I was embarrassed to think I'd let him catch me unawares like that. He kept coming in, not giving me a chance to set myself, but I covered up with my forearms and instead of backing off moved into him and pulled my knee up hard into his groin. He turned sideways and managed to block it but that left him open and I fetched him a short left hook to his right cheek that split it open along the bone.

Now I had him on the defense and as his hands went up to cover his face I dug my right to his belly, then moving in close I wrapped my arms around him and threw him to the floor. But he was up like a cat, blood streaming down the side of his face. As I went after him his hand all of sudden went to the back of his neck and the next thing I knew he had a knife in it, holding it low like he knew how to use it.

We'd both been wearing guns but he'd lost his when I threw him to the floor and his first punch had knocked all thought about mine from my mind. I wanted to kill him, all right, but with my fists not with a bullet.

We circled each other clockwise, him looking for an opening, me looking for a way to defend myself. My knife was strapped to my leg, but he sure wasn't going to give me a chance to pull up my pant leg so I could get at it. As we circled he took a swipe at me, just barely catching a bit of my shirt.

I backed toward the bar, and out of the corner of my eye I spotted a half-full bottle of whiskey sitting on the bar top. As soon as I was close enough I reached out with my right hand, grabbed the bottle by its neck, and in the same motion, like one of those baseball pitchers I'd seen once in Kansas City, I heaved it overhand right at him. He didn't have time to duck or even throw up his hand to ward it off. It caught him just above his nose and he went down like a pole-axed steer.

I went over and picked up his gun and emptied out the cartridges and tossed it down beside him. Next I picked up his knife by the haft, set my foot on the blade and snapped it off.

"I'll see ya at eight o'clock sharp," I said to Andersen, who was still standing at the bar.

I walked out into the cool night air feeling better than I had since I'd got into this mess. I hadn't come close to winning yet, but tonight, for the first time, I'd won a round.

It wasn't until I got to the hotel that I remembered our horses were still hitched out in front. Riding the roan and leading Baby I headed for the edge of town and a livery stable I'd seen riding in. I gave a dollar to the old man who was sitting outside, took the horses in, unsaddled them, forked them some hay, and walked back to the doorway. I handed the old man another dollar.

"I'm in a hurry," I said. "Can you rub 'em down?"

He pocketed the dollar, stuffed his dead pipe in his pocket, said "Yup," and headed inside whilst I hurried back to the hotel.

CHAPTER 11

WOMEN ALWAYS surprise me. Esme answered my knock wearing a dress and looking clean and refreshed. I'd expected her to be wearing jeans and the man's shirt she'd bought at the Emporium.

"Where'd you get that?" I asked.

"Get what?" she asked back. "Oh, you mean this. Dear, sweet Mrs. Weed loaned it to me. She wore it when she was younger—and thinner."

"Looks nice," I said, trying not to stare. I couldn't help but notice that she filled it out in all the right places.

"What happened to you?" she asked. "You look like you've been in a fight."

I felt the tender spot on my jaw where Fink had slugged me. "Little scuffle," I said. "Nothin' much."

I explained to her that we were to meet Andersen at the Chambers Cafe at eight o'clock.

"He's goin' to buy them cattle from Fink unless we can pursuade him that yer the owner and Fink ain't got any right to 'em. Fink says he's got written authority from you to sell 'em on your behalf."

"He couldn't have," she said. "I haven't signed any paper like that. Certainly not authorizing him to do anything. It must be a forgery."

She took out a small locket that was hanging on a gold chain she wore around her neck and flipped it open. It was a tiny watch.

"It was my mother's," she explained. "Father bought it from a Swiss jeweler who was traveling in the West. It's always kept perfect time and right now it says it's almost eight o'clock."

I felt awkward and a little shameful going down the stairs with her. Me, dirty and dusty and needing a shave and looking like I'd been in a fight. Her, clean and neat and pretty enough to do any man proud. I get this situation behind me and it was going to be different, I vowed silently.

When I found a woman who would have me I wasn't going to put her to shame. I was going to learn to read good and to write more than my name. And I was going to put some money away so I could have a spread of my own, raise some cattle, and maybe some horses. And take a bath and shave at least once a week. Whoever that woman was, I wanted her to be proud of me.

The woman I wanted would be a strong woman and a caring woman, a woman to walk beside a man, not behind him. A woman like—like Esme. But I dismissed that thought in a hurry. She'd want to do better than a rough, uncurried, uneducated puncher like me. And she could; there was no doubt in my mind about that.

"You're awfully quiet, Del," she said as we walked across the lobby.

"Thinkin'," I said.

We gotten almost to the door when it struck me. Fink or one of his men could be waiting outside. If they gunned me down—worse, if they gunned both of us down—the cattle would be his and there would be nobody to stop him from taking over the R Bar R.

I stopped and took Esme's arm.

"We're goin' out the back way," I said.

She started to protest.

"Hush, and listen up," I said. "Fink is desperate to get your cattle. He knows where we are and where we're goin' and what time we're supposed to be there. Supposin' he was to keep us from meetin' with Andersen. Andersen would think I was a phony and go ahead and buy the cows from Fink and we'd—you'd—be out in the cold."

"Oh," she said in a small voice.

We found the back entrance to the hotel, went out and down a kind of an alley 'til we came to the back of what obviously was a restaurant. The cook and a couple of helpers looked curiously at us as we entered, but I ignored them and we went on through the door to the dining room.

A waiter in a black suit came over and asked if he could help us and I said I was looking for a man named Morton Andersen.

"Little feller with short brown hair and a beard."

He led us over to a table where two men and a blond woman were seated. One was Andersen. The other man was Fink and the woman was the blonde named Irene whom we'd met, if that was the right word, at Nora's. I was pleased to see that where I'd hit Fink with the whiskey bottle there was a large bump and that both of his eyes were swole half-shut. There was a bandage, too, on his cheek that I'd split open with my fist. The look he gave me was part hatred and part triumph.

Andersen looked up. "Ah, Tackett," he said. "You know Mr. Fink so let me introduce Miss Esmeralda Rankin." He nodded at Irene.

"Yer kiddin'!" I said.

"Not at all," he replied. "She arrived in Chambers late this afternoon to personally take charge of the sale of her cattle. So it appears we have nothing to talk about. So now, if you will excuse us?"

"In a pig's eye I'll excuse you," I said angrily. "Mister, yer bein' had. That ain't Esme Rankin. This here is Miss Rankin."

He gave a shrug of resignation. "Miss Rankin," he said to Irene. "Show him the letters and things you showed me."

"What letters?" Esme demanded, shock and anger in her voice.

Irene silently handed a sheaf of letters to Andersen. He shuffled through them. "Here is one from Colonel Rankin to his daughter. Here is one from a law firm in Santa Fe to Colonel Rankin. Here is one from the dean of the Larkin School for women in Philadelphia where Miss Rankin went to school."

"You stole them. You stole them out of my desk at the ranch the same day you kidnapped me," Esme said angrily.

Andersen handed the letters back to Irene. "I've had enough of this nonsense," he said wearily. "I'm satisfied that Miss Rankin is who she says she is. The letters show it and Mr. Fink vouches for her. I have no reason to think otherwise. Now, please, we wish to continue with our dinner."

He turned away from us. We stood there undecided for a moment and finally started to leave.

"Just a minute," Esme said. "Mr. Andersen, look at this."

He looked up in annoyance as she plucked her locket from her bosom, hurriedly took it off the gold chain, and handed it to him. "Look at this," she said.

He took it from her reluctantly. "What is it you want me to see?"

"The initials," she said excitedly. "The initials."

"Look." She bent over next to him and said, "See the engraving. It says, From R.B.R.—that's my father, Reagan B. Rankin—on this side, and To L.M.R.—that's my mother, Lucinda Montoya Rankin—on this other side. And look," she flipped it open. "Here's Father's picture on the inside."

I'll hand it to Irene, she had her wits about her. "That's mine. Where did you get that?" she snapped.

"No," Esme said. "It's mine. My mother left it to me when she died.

"Mr. Andersen, I don't know who this woman is, but she is not Esmeralda Rankin. I am. And those cattle that Mr. Fink drove here are mine and he stole them. If you will give me two days I will prove it to you."

Andersen sighed heavily. "I'm tired of this. I've made my decision and I will begin loading cattle in the morning."

Esme jutted her chin out. "You do that, Mr. Andersen, and I'll see you arrested for knowingly receiving stolen property."

She took me by the arm and tugged me toward the door.

"Just a minute, Esme," I said. I looked at Fink and said, "Fink. Yer a thief and a liar and murderer."

Oh, I ached for him to go for his gun. But he just sat there and sneered at me. "I'm not armed, Tackett, but don't worry. I'll take care of you in my own good time."

"I'll watch my back," I said, allowing Esme to tug me toward the door.

We went outside and I pulled her to one side of the door and into the shadow of the building. "I'm still leery," I said. "We'll go down the back way again."

"But I'm starving," she complained.

"We'll eat," I said. "But we'll go back to the hotel first."

We went between the buildings and back to the hotel the way we'd come. Once in the lobby I asked her to wait. I went back out the rear door and eased along the side of the building until I came to the front. By the light of a nearly full moon I check up and down the street. No one. Directly across the street there was a building with a covered porch running across the width of it, throwing the building itself into deep shadow. If there was anyone there I sure couldn't see him.

But suddenly, there in the shadows a match flared and I could make out someone lighting a cigarette. He took a couple of drags on it, then dropped it on the porch floor and stepped on it. I watched a minute longer but there was no further movement.

I backed slowly away from the corner of the hotel and as soon as I knew I couldn't be seen, I headed to the back of the hotel, turned left and went past it by maybe a hundred yards.

Suddenly I was in back of a saloon. I went in the back way, strolled nonchalantly through the barroom and out through the batwing doors in front. I walked casually across the street and turned away from the man on the porch until I came to an opening between two buildings. Hurrying to the back of the buildings I turned left, this time in the direction of the hotel, which was now on the opposite side of the street.

When I came to the building directly across from the hotel I ducked into the narrow passageway between it and the building next to it and silently made my way to the front. Groping on the

135

ground I found a pebble. Still hiding along side the corner of the building I gave it a backhand fling. It landed on the porch beyond the silent watcher. When I heard it hit I leaped onto the porch and in two long strides I was on top of him. Hearing my footsteps he whirled, reaching for his gun, but it was too late; my gun was already jabbing him in the ribs.

"Don't move," I said, "and you may live a long time."

He was startled, but he put on a brave front. "What the hell do you think you're doin'?" he spat out.

"You seemed lonesome over here," I said. "Thought you might like some company."

"Go to hell," he said.

"Instead, let's me and you go over to the hotel. I want to see what you look like."

I reached around him and lifted his gun from its holster and stuck it behind my belt. Then I jabbed him in the ribs with my gun and pushed him off the porch and over to the hotel.

"Inside," I ordered. "And look natural."

As we walked into the lobby Esme saw us and started to come over but I waved her off.

"All right, you, what were you doin' over there?" I demanded.

"Go to hell," he repeated. He was a surly-looking puncher, medium height, stocky and dark haired. His nose had been broke at least once and his cheeks were pockmarked from an early case of small pox.

"I ain't done nothin'," he said. "Now git that gun out of my ribs."

"I think I'll leave it there a while," I said. "I think you and me'll go up to my room and have a talk."

I thought I caught a flicker of something in his eye at the mention of my room, but he remained poker-faced.

"Let's go, friend," I said, prodding him again. We walked across the lobby and up the stairs and to my room. I fished my key out of my pocket with my free hand and unlocked the door, standing well to one side.

"You go in first, cowboy," I said.

He didn't want to. "I don't know what's in there," he said, a touch of fear in his voice.

"Let's find out, cowboy," I said, prodding him harder.

He took hold of the knob, turned it and leaped through the doorway, shouting, "Don't shoot. It's me."

I could barely hear him over the sound of the gunfire. I saw him jerk once, twice, three times and then crumple to the floor.

"Let's get out of here," a voice said.

I heard scraping sounds, then silence. I fetched a match from my pocket, lit it, found the lamp and lighted it. The window was open and I knew that's how they'd left. I bent over the scar-faced puncher. He was dead. Quickly I taken his gun from behind my belt and jammed it into his holster.

By now there was the sound of boots in the hallway and on the stairs. Half a dozen men crowded into the hallway by the door, one wearing a badge. It said "Marshal" on it. He was a hard-faced man with cold blue eyes and narrow lips, under a bushy mustache.

"What the hell is going on here?" he demanded.

"Danged if I know, marshal," I said. "Me and my friend here was goin' into the room and someone inside opened fire on us. They went out the window yonder."

He looked intently at me. "Gimme yer gun," he ordered.

I handed it to him. He held the muzzle to his nose and sniffed. Then he spun the cylinder, shaking out all six rounds. None had been fired.

"Ain't you," he said, reloading and handing my gun back.

He bent over the dead man. "He don't look familiar. What'd you say his name was?"

"Didn't," I said. "Don't know him. Met him outside the hotel. He said he had somethin' to tell me in private. We come up here to talk."

The marshal turned to the desk clerk who had joined the group.

"Find a couple of men and get this feller down to the undertaker's. Rest of you fellers, clear out."

Then he turned back to me. "Yer Tackett, ain't ya?"

"Glory be," I said. "You got my name right. How'd you know?"

"Saw ya down in Globe a couple of years ago. Never forget a face, 'specially when a fast gun goes with it."

"Marshal," I said, "I ain't no gunfighter. I don't want to be no gunfighter. I'm here trying to stop a feller from stealin' a herd of my boss's cows, and that's all."

"Cain't hep ya," he said. "I'm hired ta keep the peace here. My authority stops at the town limits."

"Ain't expectin' help, marshal. Just want you to know I ain't here to cause trouble."

"You already brought trouble to someone," he said, gesturing at the body. "So do me a favor. Do yer business as soon as you can and get outta town."

"Glad to," I said, relieved that he wasn't trying to roust me.

Esme was still sitting in the lobby. She was pale and looked tired and worn.

"What was that shooting?" she asked. "Someone said a man had been killed."

"Wasn't me," I replied. "Let's find some food."

The desk clerk directed me to the "second best" and only other restaurant in town and we walked down to it. It wasn't fancy but the plump, middle-aged waitress was pleasant and served us with a smile.

The food was plain, but the coffee was hot and tasted good. We ate in silence. Afterward the waitress refilled our cups and we sat there sipping at it, pretty much lost in our own thoughts. Finally I asked her: "You said if Andersen would give us two days you could prove yer Esmeralda Rankin. What'd ya have in mind?"

"I have two ideas," she said. "But neither of them will do any good if he ships my cattle tomorrow. Del, isn't there anything we can do? Can't we find a judge or somebody to issue some kind of restraining order or something?"

"Look, Esme. There's a town marshal here and that's all. This ain't even the county seat and that's where you'd find the sheriff and a court. But I think I've figured a way to keep Andersen from shippin' them cattle tomorrow."

We talked for almost another hour. She didn't like my plan at first but finally agreed there wasn't anything else we could do. I didn't like hers any better because it meant a desperately long ride for me and leaving her alone for a day and a half, but, like her, I didn't have anything better to offer.

I paid the bill and we went back to the Cattlemen's Hotel. I put her in her room and waited until she'd locked her door. Then I went downstairs and got the night clerk to give me a room without any blood on the floor, and gave him a dollar to be sure and wake me up at three o'clock the next morning.

He pounded on my door at three o'clock sharp. Five minutes later I was headed for the livery stable. I roused the old man, who grumbled until I gave him a quarter. He lighted a lantern and I taken it and went back and saddled the roan. By three-thirty I was on the trail headed north.

Up ahead of me about five miles was the R Bar R herd. I galloped the roan for about twenty minutes, then slowed to trot and swung wide of the trail. A wind coming down from the north brought the smell of the herd to me before I saw it. I walked the roan softly now, until I could see the dark mass of the cattle against the sky. I dismounted and tied the roan to a little mesquite tree, taking a careful look around to make sure I'd remember where I'd left him, and set off on foot.

There had to be a couple of night guards circling the herd, keeping it calm, and I had to be careful not to be seen by them or to startle the cattle. What I was looking for was where the cavvy— the horses—were staked out. I wanted a couple of fresh horses for the ride ahead of me and I was looking in particular for Old Dobbin. That bay horse and me had rode a lot of trails together and I wanted him back.

I spotted the camp first, the glow of a camp fire and the chuck wagon, on the west side of the herd. It was at least four o'clock by now and it wouldn't be long before the cook was stirring, so I had not much time to waste. Beyond the camp was the cavvy. They wasn't expecting no trouble and nobody was on guard there. I moved quietlike among the horses, whispering soft words of reassurance, patting a neck here and a nose there. Finally I found Old Dobbin. He saw me about the same time and nickered softly. I went over and rubbed his nose, undid his tether and led him quietly away. I wished I had time to get another horse, because the roan was still tired from yesterday's long ride, but I didn't want to risk making a noise and I knew I was running out of time.

Walking quickly back to the roan I switched saddles and mounted Old Dobbin, leaving the roan still tied to the mesquite tree. Drawing my gun I jabbed my spurs in Old Dobbin's flanks, and charged the herd firing as I went and letting loose with a wild warwhoop.

I heard a cowboy holler, "What the hell," which didn't do anything to calm the cattle. Shouting and hollering I rode along the south side of the herd, reloading as I went. By now the cattle were up and stirring and it wouldn't take much to get them running. Suddenly a man on horseback loomed in front of me. I saw the flash of his gun and heard the shot, but him and me were both on moving horses and he missed. I charged on by him, slashing at him with the barrel of my gun as I raced by. I felt the barrel hit him across the face and heard his agonized scream and then I was beyond him, shooting and hollering.

The cattle on my side of the herd were now up and looking for a place to run. As I wheeled Old Dobbin and came back, reloading again, they began heading west, toward the camp. Shooting and yelling, I hurried them along and they quickly broke into a run. We were close enough to the camp now so I could hear shouts and shots as they sought to stop or turn the herd. But it was too late. The whole herd was running now and the south edge of it went tearing through the camp, lumbered through the picketed horses, and ran wildly toward the desert.

I doubled back, found the roan, untied him, and the three of us—me and Old Dobbin and the roan—took off at a mile-eating trot, headed north for Nora and the ranch.

Halfway to Nora I switched my saddle to the roan and after fifteen miles switched it back again to Old Dobbin. I rode into Nora shortly after noon, dropped the roan off at the livery stable, picked up a hammer-headed dun, and leading Old Dobbin headed for the R Bar R.

I was almost there before I remembered that Jump Cassidy, Red, and the other rustler might be hanging around if they hadn't already taken the ranch. If that had happened then I was out of luck and so was Esme. The deed to the ranch was hidden in a wall safe in the living room and if they were there there was no way I could blast them out without help. And I didn't have none.

I wished then that I really was a Sackett. I could gather my kinfolk around me and together we could save Esme and the ranch and the herd. But I wasn't no Sackett, just a big, old mountain boy from the high Sierras of California, without no kinfolk at all that I knew of. Well, I would do the best I could and if that meant going down fighting, that was that. A man can't do no more than his best and I aimed to give it my best shot.

I was careful now, looking at every bush and tree and rock to see if there was a man behind it. There wasn't. I was almost into the ranch yard when a bullet raised dust in front of me and I heard a shot. The bullet wasn't meant to hit me, so I stopped and yelled, "Hello, the house!"

Blackie raised his head above the parapet that ran around all four sides of the roof of the ranch house.

"What the hell are you doin' here?" he shouted. "Come on in."

I rode on in and dismounted stiffly. Lew and Mary Lou and Jack Sears all came to the door and Beauty squeezed by them and bounded down the steps and licked my hand.

"Didn't think you'd have the guts to come back," Sears greeted me.

I pushed by them into the house and sprawled into the big

leather chair in the living room. I was exhausted. I'd ridden seventy miles in less than twelve hours and one hundred and twenty miles in a 24-hour period.

They had a hundred questions and so did I. It turned out that after Lew had arrived back at the ranch Jump Cassidy had ridden boldly up, apparently hoping he wouldn't be recognized. But Blackie had spotted him and when he got close he'd warned him off with a couple of shots. At the same time Sears had caught the other two trying to sneak up in back of the house and had opened fire. He thought he'd winged Red, but wasn't sure. After that they'd kept one man on lookout on the roof and had taken turns sleeping, but there had been no further evidence of the trio.

I told them I'd come for the deed to the ranch so we could prove to Andersen that Esme was the rightful owner. They sent up a lonely cheer when I told them how I'd stampeded the herd.

I hadn't eaten since the night before so Mary Lou rustled up some grub, but I fell asleep with my head on the table before I finished. They roused me just long enough to take me to a bed and pull my boots off. I was in a dead sleep when they woke me up four hours later. I went out and splashed water on my face and sat down to a dinner of beans and beef that Mary Lou had saved for me.

Lew announced that he was going back with me, in case I fell asleep on the way. He'd already saddled the four best horses in the corral. I would have liked to take Old Dobbin but I didn't want to run him to death. I wanted him there when we came back.

I went into the living room and took down the painting of Esme's mother that hung over the fireplace. I'd never really looked at it close before. She had been a beautiful woman with dark Spanish features, a sensuous mouth, and a straight nose. Her eyes and hair were black. It was easy to see where Esme had gotten her looks and coloring.

Behind the picture was a small wall safe. Using the combination Esme had given me, I opened it and looked inside. On top of everything was Ma's diary. I'd forgotten all about it after I'd tried to read it and apparently Esme had picked it up and put it there for safekeeping. Under the diary was a bundle of papers.

I called Mary Lou in and, flushing with embarrassment, said, "Mary Lou, I don't read too good. Which one of these papers is the deed?"

She didn't say anything, just took the papers and shuffled through them until she found the deed. It was in a heavy, brown envelope and I taken it and tucked it inside my shirt.

"Yer a good lady," I said and leaned over and kissed her lightly on the cheek.

She blushed and tears began to form at the corners of her eyes. "And you're a good man, Del Tackett," she murmered.

I taken a bait of grub she'd packed for us and Ma's diary and went out to where Lew was waiting. I put the food and diary in my saddlebags, gave Beauty a pat on the head, and mounted up.

"Take care of things," I said to Blackie and Sears, "especially Mary Lou."

Sears gave me a funny look, but didn't say nothing but "So long," which Blackie and Mary Lou echoed, and shortly before midnight Lew and me headed out at a trot on the long trail that led south to Chambers.

We changed horses just the other side of Nora and again half way between Nora and Chambers. We passed the R Bar R herd, which had mostly been rounded up again, on the west side of the trail, and shortly after noon, cantered across the bridge and into Chambers. Dropping the horses off at the livery stable we headed up the dusty, unpaved street to the Cattlemen's Hotel.

CHAPTER 12

WE CROSSED THE hotel lobby, went up the stairs and down the hallway to Esme's room. I knocked, but there was no answer. We waited a minute and went back downstairs.

"You seen Miss Rankin?" I asked the desk clerk.

"Nope," he said. "She hasn't been downstairs today."

A feeling of dread shot through me. What if something had happened to Esme when I was gone? I kicked myself for having left her alone, yet what else could I have done. She certainly could not have endured the long ride I'd just come off of.

"Bring your pass key and come with us," I told him.

Lew and I headed upstairs with the clerk trailing behind. At Esme's room I knocked once again. Again, no answer. Taking the key from the clerk I unlocked the door. Esme lay face down across her unmade bed, dressed only in her nightgown. I crossed the room to her in two quick strides. There was a large bump on the side of her head and blood on the coverlet.

"Oh, God, don't let her be dead," I prayed silently. Just then she uttered a low groan and moved her head slightly.

"Thank God," I said aloud.

Which was as much praying and thanks giving as I'd done in most of my life.

"Is there a doctor in this town?" I asked the clerk.

"Only old Doc Dickery, and he ain't always sober."

"Get him," I rasped. "Now!"

He hurried from the room.

I gently turned Esme over and Lew helped me straighten her

145

out on the bed. I pulled the half of the coverlet she wasn't lying on over her as much to protect her modesty as to keep her warm.

In a minute she opened her eyes and gazed around blankly. Then she struggled to sit up. I pressed her back down gently.

"Don't move, honey," I said. "Me and Lew're here. Everything's going to be all right."

She lay back down and closed her eyes.

"Oh, Del," she murmured, "I'm so glad you're here. You always seem to come just when I need you most."

By this time Lew had brought a towel and a basin of water. I dampened the towel and lay it across her forehead.

Not knowing what else to do—I ain't no sawbones—I drew up the only chair in the room and sat beside the bed, holding Esme's hand, as much for my comfort as for hers. Lew slouched against the wall by the door and every now and then stepped out to see if the doctor was coming. A few minutes later the clerk showed up with the doctor in tow. I could see what the clerk had meant. He was a fat little man with a red nose and a lot of broken little veins in his cheeks. His eyes could have been substituted for a flag. They were a washed-out blue and the whites were crisscrossed with fine red veins. He had shoulder-length white hair and a bushy white mustache, stained yellow from much tobacco smoke. But he seemed sober.

He came in with his black bag which he set on the floor beside the bed. He stuck out his hand for me to shake, which I did. "Doctor Hickman Dickery," he introduced himself. "My friends call me Hickory. What seems to be the trouble?"

"Don't rightly know, Doc," I said. "But looks like someone broke into the lady's room and hit her on the head."

He kind of nudged me to one side and bent over her. With a chubby finger he pulled back one of her eyelids. That got her attention. She pushed his arm aside and tried to sit up. He put one arm under her back and helped her. She looked around and seeing herself under the watchful gaze of four relatively strange men, pulled the coverlet up over her bosom. Holding it there with one hand she reached the other one up and gently touched the bump on the side of her head.

"It hurts," she said.

"Be a miracle if it didn't," Doc Dickery said. "Let me take a look at it."

With suprisingly gentle hands he pulled her hair to one side. The bump was large and already beginning to discolor. The skin had been torn open, rather than cut, but she had bled only a little.

Doc Dickery took a pair of scissors from his bag and carefully cut the hair from around the wound.

"I don't think we need to sew that up," he said. "I'm going to put a little salve on it—most folks use iodine but that stings too much so I use this linament. It's good for horses and people both—and then I'll put a little bandage on it. You rest until tomorrow and I think you'll be all right. If you're not, send Oscar here," he nodded at the hotel clerk, "to find me. He knows where to look."

He worked as he talked and it wasn't long before he was finished.

"I'll have them add the fee to your hotel bill," he said, snapping his bag shut.

"Gentlemen." He shook hands all around and went out the door.

"I hear he was a big-time doctor back East somewhere until the liquor got to him," Oscar said as he, too, headed for the door.

Esme lay back down on the bed and I managed to pull some covers over her.

"Can you tell us what happened?" I asked.

"I'm not sure," she said. "I was tired so I slept late this morning. I was awakened by a knock on the door. Somebody—a man—said he had a message for me from you. When I unlocked the door he pushed his way in, grabbed me and threw me on the bed. When I struggled he hit me with his gun and that's all I remember."

"Did he say anything?" I asked.

"He said something about my locket—oh, my locket!" She put her hand to her throat. "It's gone! My locket is gone. Why? Why?"

"Why because," I said. "If they have your locket it's one more piece of proof that that Irene woman is really you."

"But why? They've already convinced Mr. Andersen."

"They want more'n your cattle. They want your ranch, too. They ain't got the deed so they need proof that Irene is really you in case anyone was to question their ownership."

Her face fell. "Oh," she said. Then she brightened. "The deed. Did you get the deed?"

"Sure thing," I said, pulling the envelope from under my shirt and handing it to her.

"That's wonderful," she said. "Now if the wires have just come in."

"I'll go see," I said. "Lew, we best let Miss Esme get some sleep. You stay here and watch and I'll be back quicklike."

I went down the stairs and grabbed the clerk again. "Two things. Find some coffee and maybe some grub and get it upstairs to the feller watchin' the lady's door."

"She all right?" he asked.

"Yep," I said. "She's sleepin'. Now tell me. Which way's the railroad station?"

On the way to the station, someone yelled "Tackett." I stopped and the marshal came up.

"Thought you'd done me a favor and left town," he said.

"Did. But had to come back. Be gone fer good in a day or two.

"By the way, marshal, there's a lady over at the hotel named Esmeralda Rankin. Somebody busted into her room a while back, knocked her out and stole a locket her ma had left her."

"I'll check into it," he said. "But it won't do much good unless she can find the person who took her locket. I ain't got the time or the know-how to be a detective. I'm here mainly to keep the peace. You point the man out who hit her and I'll arrest him for ya."

"Thanks," I said. "For nothin'," I added to myself, turning away and heading again for the station.

But it was my day for bumping into people. I ran into Andersen coming out of the Chambers Cafe. He saw me and stopped. "Your lady friend got the two days she asked for," he said. "Because somebody—I wonder who—stampeded that herd."

"Do tell," I grinned. "You get 'em rounded up again? Anyone hurt in the stampede?"

"One man killed," he said grimly. "Another man hurt pretty bad where someone slashed him across the face with a pistol barrel."

"Wages of sin," I said. "Folks ought not to go stealin' other folks' cattle."

"I'm loading first thing tomorrow," he said. "So if you got any proof those cattle are yours you had better get it to me today."

I hurried on to the railroad station and found the station master who was also the telegraph operator, the janitor and the handyman.

I could tell he was the telegraph operator because he was wearing a green-visored eyeshade. He was a thin man, about forty with a wad of tobacco in his cheek and a spittoon, which he seldom managed to hit, on the floor by his desk.

"You got any wires here for Miss Esmeralda Rankin?" I asked.

He shuffled through the papers on his desk and picked up three.

"Yep," he said. "Sign for 'em here."

Laboriously I signed my name and put the telegrams in my shirt.

"Ain't ya going to read 'em?" he asked with just the hint of a sneer. He'd seen me drawing my name and figured pretty quick that I wasn't much on reading.

"I'll read you from the good book, mister, you get smart with me," I snarled.

"No offense, mister," he said, turning pale.

I stomped out the door and back to the hotel. Damn, but I was going to have to take some time and learn to read and write a sight better than I could now.

I went on up to Esme's room. Lew was sitting in a chair next to the door drinking a cup of coffee.

"Sure tastes good after that long ride," he said.

All of a sudden I was thirsty and hungry and tired, especially tired. I been too busy and too angry to pay much attention to the wounds and bumps on my head, but now that I stopped to think about it, I still had a dull headache. What I needed was about twenty-four hours steady of sleep and then a week of just lying around eating and sleeping and maybe talking to a pretty girl if I could find one to talk to. Not just any pretty girl, I admitted to myself, but a particular one, and she was just on the other side of the door I was looking at.

I knocked and Esme's sleepy voice called, "Come in."

After she sat up and pulled the covers around her I handed her the telegrams. One of them was from the law firm of Bush, Walker, Herbert and George in Santa Fe. She read it to me:

PER YOUR REQUEST THE FOLLOWING IS A DESCRIPTION OF ES-MERALDA SYLVIA RANKIN STOP HEIGHT 5 FEET FOUR INCHES STOP BLACK HAIR STOP BROWN EYES STOP RED BIRTHMARK ON FRONT OF RIGHT SHOULDER STOP 22 YEARS OLD STOP MISS RANKIN LIKE HER FATHER BEFORE HER IS A VALUED CLIENT STOP (SIGNED) NEAL WALKER FOR BUSH, WALKER, HERBERT AND GEORGE ATTORNEYS AT LAW STOP

The next wire she read to me was from Lucinda Fisher, the dean of women at the Larkin School for Women in Philadelphia:

TO WHOM IT MAY CONCERN STOP MISS ESMERALDA SYLVIA RANKIN WAS GRADUATED FROM THE LARKIN SCHOOL IN 1886 STOP SHE IS FIVE FEET FOUR INCHES TALL STOP WEIGHS APPROXIMATELY 120 LBS STOP HAS BROWN EYES AND BLACK HAIR STOP. HAS BIRTHMARK ON RIGHT SHOULDER STOP (SIGNED) LUCINDA FISHER DEAN STOP

The third wire read:

HAVE KNOWN ESMERALDA RANKIN ALL HER LIFE STOP CAN VOUCH FOR HER STOP SHE HAS BROWN EYES BLACK HAIR ABOUT 5 FEET 4 OR 5 INCHES STOP CONTACT ME IF FURTHER DETAILS NEEDED STOP (SIGNED) GENERAL PHILIP SHERIDAN US ARMY (RET)STOP

"Oh Del," Esme said. "Isn't this wonderful. This proves that that woman is an imposter and a fraud. When Mr. Andersen sees these he'll have to admit the cattle are mine."

"That's true," I said. "Unless he's in cahoots with Fink and his gang. And even if he's not, there's no way Lew and me can take on that bunch and get yer cattle back. We got to figure somethin' out. And right now I'm too tired to think straight. Let me get a couple of hours sleep and we'll talk some more."

She reached out and took my hand. "You get some sleep, Del. We'll talk later."

I went out and rousted Lew who was sleeping in his chair which was tilted back against the wall.

"I gotta get some sleep," I said. "You stay awake for a couple of hours, then get me up and I'll come and relieve you."

He nodded and I went on down to my room, crawled on my bed, and fell asleep without even bothering to take off my boots. When I awoke I was surprised because I hadn't been sleeping very long. Maybe it was the smell that bothered me; I hadn't had a bath or a shave in over a week now. I went downstairs and found the clerk who for a quarter quickly arranged for hot water, soap, and a towel. I washed about an inch of dirt and sweat off of me and, feeling a lot cleaner, headed for the barbershop where I got me a shave and a haircut.

I'd left Lew for more than two hours but I still had one more errand to run. At the general store I found some underwear, socks, a light blue shirt, and pair of brown jeans.

Lew was getting restless by the time I returned, but I taken ten minutes more to shed my trail dirty clothes and put on the clean ones. Then I went down to Esme's room and told Lew to go get some sleep.

"Ya look so purty and smell so good I could almost kiss ya," he said as he left.

I felt pretty much the same way myself. I knocked on Esme's door and waited when she said, "Just a moment."

It taken longer than that but eventually she opened the door.

She was dressed to go out and her black hair was brushed to at least partly hide her bandage. As usual I had trouble to keep from staring at her.

"Come in, Del," she said. "My, but don't you look nice. I hardly recognized you."

She said she was feeling fine, although she admitted her head was aching.

"Perhaps if I had a cup of coffee it would help," she said.

"I could use some, too," I admitted.

We walked down to the restaurant we'd been at the first night we were in town. She held on to my arm as we walked and it had been a long time since I'd felt the way I did: Strong and protective and, I suddenly realized, in love. I shook my head in disgust and she said, "What is it, Del?"

"Nothin'," I said. But I knew better. Here I was a big, homely, uneducated mountain boy who didn't know much about anything but mining and guns and horses, who didn't have any money except what I had in my pocket and wasn't likely to get any. Here I was, falling in love with the daughter of an army colonel, who'd been to fancy schools back east, who owned a big ranch and who was the prettiest girl I'd ever seen.

Best thing for me to do was drift along as soon as we got the herd back and I had run Reggie Fink out of the country. That stopped me again. I wasn't going to run Fink out of the country and I knew it. Sooner or later there was going to be a showdown between him and me and one of us wasn't going to walk away from it. Either way I knew I'd be leaving—leaving Esme behind—but I didn't know yet whether I'd be on a horse or in a coffin.

It could easy be the latter. Reggie Fink, alias Ray Failor, was a fast man with a gun, maybe faster than me. Not only that but he liked killing people while with me it was different. There was never yet a time I had killed that I didn't feel at least some regret. Oh, I didn't lose much sleep when I killed a man like Evan Stevens or did it in self-defense, but still I'd never gotten over being bothered at the thought of taking a human life.

We went into the little restaurant and the plump waitress gave us a table over in a corner. We both ordered coffee and a piece of apple pie which was almost as good as what Esme had served that first night at the R Bar R. I'd been giving a lot of thought to our earlier conversation but hadn't come up with any brainstorm.

Finally I said, "Esme, I think we got to take one thing at a time. We can't worry about gettin' the herd back from Fink until we make certain Morton Andersen don't buy it and ship it. He does that and it seems to me we wind up losers.

"Seems to me the best thing for us to do is find Andersen and show him the proof of who you are, along with the deed to the R Bar. If he still won't listen maybe you can threaten to get them lawyers of yours to bring suit against him and his company. They wouldn't like the idea of havin' to pay you for the herd after he's already paid Fink.

"Why don't we go back to the hotel and see if we can find him. If he ain't there then I'll see if I can run him down and bring him back to the hotel."

"But what if he's with Fink and that awful woman?" Esme asked, shivering a little, even though it was warm in the cafe.

I shrugged. "There's gonna be a showdown sooner or later so it might as well be sooner."

A voice in back of me said, "Howdy, Tackett. You stayin' out of trouble?"

I looked around. It was the town marshal.

"Howdy, marshal," I said. "Pull up a chair and set a bit. I'd introduce you to the lady but I never caught yer name."

He swept off his hat and bowed toward Esme. "Howdy ma'am. Name of Jack Simpson. I'm the town marshal hereabouts."

"This here is Miss Esmeralda Rankin. Owns the R Bar R up north of Nora."

Simpson's face darkened. "Hold on a minute. There's somethin' fishy goin' on here. I ran into a cattle buyer name of Morton Andersen an hour or so back and he introduced me to a blond lady he was with. Said she was Esmeralda Rankin. One of you is lyin'."

I half rose out of my chair in anger, but sank down again. He was right. Someone was lying. It was Fink and the blond Irene but Simpson had no way of knowing that. I looked at Esme. She had turned red and her full lips had narrowed.

"Mr. Simpson," she said. "I am not a liar. Let me show you some evidence of who I am." She opened her purse and brought out the three telegrams that had come in earlier. Simpson read them carefully, moving his lips with each word.

"General Sheridan," he said. "Had an uncle who fought under him. Little feller, but one hell—pardon me, ma'am—heck of a leader."

Silently Esme handed him the deed to the R Bar R. "It hardly seems likely that I would have this if I weren't the owner," she said quietly.

"Ma'am," Simpson said. "Seems like I owe you an apology."

"You had no way of knowing," Esme said graciously.

"Marshal," I said. "I know yer jurisdiction stops at the town limits, but here in town yer job is to keep the peace, right?"

He nodded.

"Marshal, I got a hunch that once Andersen agrees that Miss Esme is the rightful owner of them cows Reggie Fink is holdin' out near the loadin' pens there's goin' to be hell to pay around here. Fink ain't goin' to take losin' them cattle lyin' down. If he comes after me there's going to be some shootin' 'less you can stop him first.

"You know Fink?" I asked.

"Seen him around," he replied.

"His other name is Ray Failor," I said.

"Can't be. Failor's dead. Killed down in east Texas."

"That's what he wants folks to think. But he ain't. You know Nora's place up there at Nora?"

He nodded. "Been there a time or two. Oops, sorry, ma'am."

Esme blushed, but didn't say anything.

"Well," I continued. "She's Fink's ma. She had him afore she ever got married. Matter of fact she never did get married. She told me all about him. On top of that, that blond woman who claims to be Esme works for Nora, or did anyway."

"Ray Failor," he mused. "Supposed to be as fast as Doc Holliday or John Wesley Hardin. Sure as hell faster'n me."

He looked at me. "Got any ideas?"

"Yeah," I said. "Why don't you throw him in jail. Get a couple of deputies and when he comes into town again, if he's not already here, arrest him. Throw him in jail for a few days. Any trumped-up charge'll do. Without him that crew of his won't be much. Probably even load the cows for Andersen, if he'll pay 'em."

"What about you?" he asked.

"Well, first me and Miss Esme have to find Andersen and show him our proof of ownership. Once he agrees to that I won't have nothin' to do until the cows are loaded. But I'll be around in case you need someone to keep Fink's men off your back. Got a hand with me, too. Name of Lew Haight. He'll help. Come to think of it you might want to use him for one of yer deputies. I'll send him around."

I turned to Esme. "Make sense to you?"

She nodded yes. Simpson pushed back his chair and put on his hat. "I'll keep an eye out for Fink. You watch yer back.

"Pleasure to meet you, ma'am."

"Well, at least we got the law on our side," I said. "Why don't we go see if we can find Andersen."

I paid the check and we strolled back to the hotel. It was almost dark by now and the lights had gone on in all the buildings. It was a beautiful evening, just cool enough, and a nearly full moon was rising in the east. Esme hugged my arm close to her as we walked and I had to fight off the urge to stop and take her in my arms.

Instead, I said, "Soon as we get this behind us I'll be driftin' along."

It caught her off guard and before she thought she said, "Del, you can't. I need you."

I stopped right there in the middle of that board sidewalk, swung her around so she was facing me and taken her by both arms. Her lips parted a little and there was a light in her eyes I hadn't seen before. I felt her kind of move toward me. In the barest nick of time I dropped my arms.

"You shouldn't ought to say things like that," I said gruffly.

She didn't say anything, just looked at me for a long moment. Finally I taken her by the arm and started off again for the hotel. That had been a narrow escape for both of us. I knowed it, even if she didn't.

CHAPTER 13

THE DESK CLERK told me that Andersen had a room on the first floor in the back so Esme and I headed that way. We'd been silent the last half of the way to the hotel, busy with our own thoughts. I sneaked a look at her every now and then but she continued to look straight ahead, her face grave and unsmiling.

We were lucky. Andersen was just leaving his room when we arrived. He didn't seem happy to see us and was even more unhappy when I told him we needed to see him. Reluctantly he led us back into his room. It was a large room with one end of it set up as a sort of parlor with a sofa and chairs. He motioned to us to be seated.

"I really don't see what we have to talk about," he said, "so please be brief. I have other business to attend to."

Esme silently handed him the three wires. He read each one and then reread them. When he had finished she handed him the deed to R Bar R. After a minute he looked up.

"Seems like I've been mistaken," he said. "I'm not often fooled this way. That Fink is an impressive man."

"He's Eastern-educated," I said. "Puts on fancy airs when he wants to. But watch out for him. He's a dangerous man."

"Is he really Ray Failor?" he asked.

"Yup," I said.

He studied his fingernails intently for a bit. Finally he asked, "What would you like me to do?"

Esme looked at me questioningly.

"Buy the herd," I said. "Make the check out to Esmeralda Rankin."

157

He interrupted. "It's not a check, it's gold certificates. He insisted on it. Said checks weren't practical out here. The bank is holding the money. We're to meet there when it opens tomorrow at 9 a.m. He was to give me a bill of sale and I was to have the bank turn the money over to him."

"Mr. Andersen," Esme said, "I will be at the bank at 9 in the morning with a bill of sale for those cattle. You can then instruct the bank to pay me instead of Mr. Fink. With the evidence I have here I don't think there is much he can do about it."

Suddenly her voice trailed off and she put a hand to her forehead.

"Are you all right, Miss?" Andersen asked looking at her carefully. It was then that he noticed her bandage.

"You're hurt," he said. "What happened to you?"

"I'm all right," Esme said. "I just got dizzy there for a moment."

I broke in. "Remember that locket Esme showed you last night? Some feller broke into her room, knocked her out, and stole it. Thought they were takin' her last bit of proof about who she is."

"I was sure wrong," Andersen said, standing up. "I hope some day I can make it up to you. In the meantime I'll expect to see you at the bank at 9 a.m."

We left and went up to Esme's room. "I'm afraid I'm not as strong as I thought I was," she said. "I would like to lie down for a while before we have dinner."

"Lock yer door," I said. "And don't open to nobody 'less'n you know who it is."

I waited until I heard the lock click, then I went off to get Lew. He was still asleep, but came wide awake in a hurry and we went off to find the marshal. He was sitting in his office with his feet on a spur-scarred desk.

"Howdy," he said, not bothering to get up.

I introduced him to Lew. After he shook hands he dug around in a drawer until he found a badge that said "Deputy" on it.

"You swear to uphold the peace and arrest anyone who breaks the law?" he asked.

"Yup," Lew said, catching the badge that Simpson tossed at him and pinning it on. "What next?"

"Marshal," I said, "whyn't we do this the easy way? No sense in startin' a ruckus tonight if you don't have to. Fink is meetin' Andersen—the cattle buyer—at the bank at nine in the mornin'. You and Lew can be waitin' there and you can arrest him then. If you hold him for a couple of days Andersen can get his cattle loaded and out of here and me and Esme and Lew can be back at the ranch.

"We'll figure out what to do from there."

"Suits me," Simpson said. "See you in the morning."

The blond woman, Irene, was sitting in the lobby when we got back to the hotel. I went over and stared at her and she looked back at me with a kind of sneer. If she'd been a man I would have hit her.

"Yer out of place here. This ain't Nora's," I said.

"You're out of place, too, cowboy," she said coldly. "This isn't the rock you crawled out from under."

She got me there. I longed for a snappy comeback, but one wouldn't come. I started to turn and walk away when I noticed a thin, gold chain around her neck and dipping down into her bosom.

"What you got hangin' on that chain?" I asked.

"None of your damn business," she answered.

"Irene," I said. "I know what you got there. And before this ruckus is over I aim to have it back if I have to rip it offn you."

"Fink will kill you first," she said. "Here, take a look"—she drew Esme's locket out from between her breasts—"That's the last time you'll ever see it."

She dropped it back, and glared at me defiantly. I walked back to where Lew was waiting and we went on upstairs.

"Better take that badge off for now, Lew," I said. "No use in callin' attention to it and you."

It was early yet so I figured to give Esme another hour to rest before we went to dinner. I told Lew to meet me in my room in an hour and went in, pulled my boots off, and lay back, intending to take a nap. But sleep wouldn't come.

A jumble of thoughts ran through my mind. Esme . . . the one girl I'd ever really wanted and never could have. Ma . . . I missed her. Even if I hadn't seen her for all those years, at least I'd known she was there. Ma's diary . . . I knew I was going to have to learn to read if I was ever going to find out about myself. Reggie Fink . . . He was Esme's half brother, yet I knew I was going to have to kill him. And from him my mind wandered to all the other men I'd killed, even though I hadn't wanted to. Most of 'em bad men who'd had it coming, but still, I would've avoided it if I could have. Killing wasn't never going to be a casual thing with me, I knew, and I was grateful.

A knock on the door aroused me from my reverie. It hadn't been nearly an hour so I knew it wasn't Lew. I got up, took my pistol from its holster, and called, "Come in."

It was Simpson. He stopped short when he saw the gun. "Expectin' someone else?" he said, just a bit amused.

"Never know, marshal. Ain't everybody in this town is friendly."

"I've some bad news," he said.

I just looked at him and he drew a telegram from his shirt pocket. "Here, read this," he said, reaching it out to me.

"Read it to me," I said, trying to act nonchalant. He looked at me kind of funny, and I knew he knew I couldn't read. He wasn't the quickest reader in the world, either, but he managed to fight his way through it. It said:

PER YOUR INQUIRY RAY FAILOR KILLED IN EAST TEXAS 1884 STOP REGINALD FINK NOT WANTED IN NEW MEXICO OR BY U.S. GOVERNMENT STOP.

It was signed by the United States marshal in Santa Fe.

"What does that mean?" I asked.

"Means there's nothin' I can do for you here. You'll have to handle Fink by yourself and you'll have to abide by the law here in Chambers when you do it."

"He's a cattle thief and a crook and a killer," I said hotly. "And yer just gonna stand by and let him get away with it."

"That may be true," he said. "But you ain't got enough proof for me to put him in jail. If he breaks the law or disturbs the peace I'll arrest him. Otherwise, he's your problem."

He stood up to go. "Same goes for you. Break the law or disturb the peace and I'll arrest you. And, by the way, tell Lew to drop that badge by. I just fired him."

I was mad clear through. "Shut the door when you go out," I snarled.

Forcing myself to be calm, I lay back down on the bed with my arms folded under my head. What now? Well, I knew what now. Barring a miracle there was going to be a showdown tomorrow at the Chambers bank and someone was likely to be killed. I was scared for Esme. She had to be there to give Andersen the bill of sale and identify herself to the banker. I'd be with her, of course, and so would Lew.

Fink would be there with Irene who would try to pass herself off as the real Esme Rankin. Who else he would have, if anyone, I had no idea. If there was to be a shooting showdown I had to make certain I could get Esme out of the way first.

I went and found Lew and told him the situation.

"This ain't yer fight," I told him. "Whyn't you drop that badge off at the marshal's office and clear out? Ain't nobody payin' you to get killed."

He flushed in anger. "I told you before, I ride for the brand. Me and Blackie, both. I'll be there in the mornin'."

"Thanks," I said. "Look, you go waken Esme and take her over to the Chambers restaurant. I got a man to see and I'll meet the two of you there in a bit."

I went hunting for Morton Andersen. He wasn't in his room and he wasn't in either restaurant so I headed for the saloons. He wasn't in the first one, but Jump Cassidy was. Dang! I stopped short, not looking for a fight, but he saw me.

"Howdy, Tackett," he said with a sneering grin.

"Yer a long way from the Lazy A," I said. "You huntin' trouble?"

He chuckled mirthlessly. "Not tonight. Boss has a little job for me in the morning, guardin' his back at a deal he's got cookin' at the bank. After that if you want trouble I'll be around."

"I ain't lookin' for trouble with you, Jump," I said. "My fight's with Fink. But if you wanna get mixed up in it it's yer tough luck."

Deliberately I turned my back on him and walked out the door. He was a killer and a gun for hire but despite his reputation I'd decided he was too proud to shoot a man in the back. Beside's I'd seen Simpson sitting at a table in the corner.

Andersen was in the third saloon I went into. He was standing alone at the bar. I crowded in next to him and ordered a whiskey. "Need to talk to you," I said.

We picked up our drinks and headed for a corner table.

"There's gonna be trouble in the mornin'," I said.

I proceeded to tell him about the wire Simpson had gotten from the U.S. marshal and Simpson's contention that there was nothing he could do about Fink.

"Until he got that wire he was plannin' to be at the bank in the mornin' to arrest Fink," I said. "Now he won't be. That means there'll just be you and the banker, Fink's people and us. And I'll bet my bottom dollar there's gonna be a showdown right there.

"You said earlier you owed Esme. Well, if it looks like there's gonna be shootin' I want you to get her out of the way real fast.

"If I'm killed maybe you can lend her a hand a mite until she gets straightened around."

"I said I owe her and I do," he said. "I'll do what you ask."

Esme and Lew was already seated when I got to the Chambers restaurant.

"My half brother and that Irene woman just left," Esme said bitterly. "I don't understand him. You'd think what happened between father and that terrible Nora was my fault."

"It ain't that," I said. "It don't matter to him whose fault it is. He just thinks you've got something that's rightly his, at least half of it. And he wants his share."

"But why couldn't he have come and talked about it? If he has proof that Father is his father, too, I would have been willing to share, or to buy out his half, or even let him buy me out, for that matter."

"There's more," I said. "He's twisted, Esme. He may be yer half brother but there's bad blood in him from somewhere. He's got an evil streak in him. Besides, we don't know for sure he's yer half brother. He may think he is, but like you and me he only has Nora's word for it."

I turned to Lew. "There's gonna be trouble at the bank tomorrow mornin'. I can smell it. Jump Cassidy's in town. I run into him while I was lookin' for Andersen. Said he didn't want no trouble now because he's gotta be with Fink at the bank in the morning. If there's to be fightin' I want it to be between me and Fink. Yer job is to keep Cassidy out of it, but be careful; he's a fast man with a gun."

"I'll keep an eye on him," Lew said.

"Esme," I said, "I'd be happier if you wasn't there, but you gotta be. I don't see no way around it. But at the first sign of gun trouble I want you outta the way real quick. I talked to Andersen a bit ago. He says he'll watch out for you."

Supper came and it was maybe the best food I'd ever eaten. I'd heard they had a French chef who'd come over to the States from Paris and had drifted west, but that didn't mean anything to me until I ate his grub. The condemned man ate a hearty meal, I thought, and sat back to enjoy it.

I was up late for me the next morning and Lew and I were just going downstairs heading for a cup of coffee at the second best restaurant when we heard Esme call for us to wait. She joined us and the three of us went out into the sunshine of a cloudless early June morning. It was still cool but you could feel summer coming on. We crowded into the little cafe and sat three of us at a two-person table. One of those big Regulator school clocks hung on the wall was just ticking its way to 8:30. Whoever owned the cafe must have brought it west with him or bought it from someone who had.

The plump, middle-aged waitress who'd waited on me before came over and took our order. Coffee for all of us but none of us felt much like eating. Esme had noticed the clock, too, and asked the waitress about it. She surprised me.

"My husband and I own this cafe," she said. "We came out here right after the Civil War and the clock was one of the pieces of furniture we managed to bring from the East. We started this cafe about ten years ago after we went broke trying to raise cattle. He's the cook, which is what he had been back East, and I act as the waitress. It's a lovely clock, isn't it? A lot of people ask about it."

We sat drinking our coffee and not saying much until the big hand was on twelve and the little hand was on nine. "It's nine o'clock," Esme said.

"I can tell time," I said shortly, and was immediately sorry. I knew I'd gotten real sensitive about not hardly being able to read, but I had no right to take it out on Esme.

She flushed a little but didn't say anything and I mumbled a "sorry" as we headed for the door.

The banker had just unlocked the door when we arrived at the bank and the others were already inside. Lew went in first, then Esme, and I went in last, touching my gun as I went to make sure it was loose in its holster. This was the showdown, and I knew it.

They heard us coming and turned to see who it was. They were all there, Fink, Irene and Jump Cassidy, Andersen and the banker, who's name, I'd been told, was Bofa Levy. He was what you'd expect a banker to look like—about 50, stout, and wearing a gold chain across the vest that held his stomach in.

He looked askance at us and started to speak but stopped when Morton Andersen said quietly, "It's all right."

"What the hell do you mean, it's all right?" Fink demanded. "What are these people doin' here anyway?"

164

Esme looked at him steadily. "I have sold Mr. Andersen my cattle and I am here to be paid," she said.

"Damn you," he said, looking at me. Then he stopped and I could see him grow calm and cold. And I knew that here was a really dangerous man.

He switched his gaze to Andersen. "What's this all about, Andersen?" he asked.

Andersen looked nervous but he held his ground. "Miss Rankin here—" he gestured at Esme—"has shown me irrefutable proof of her identity and her ownership of the R Bar R ranch. She tells me she has made out a bill of sale for her cattle and when she gives it to me I will instruct Mr. Levy to turn the money I have deposited with him over to her."

Irene spoke up. "You saw my proof of identify and my letter to Mr. Fink authorizing him to round up and sell the cattle on my behalf."

"Whoever you are, ma'am, you're a fraud. Miss Rankin has shown me wires from three sources describing her and identifying her. You do not meet their description and I doubt that you have a birthmark on the front of your right shoulder."

I was keeping a careful watch on Fink but out of the corner of my eye I saw Irene instinctively look at her right shoulder.

"Show us your birthmark, Irene," I said, never taking my eyes off Fink.

"Go to hell, Tackett," she spat out.

"Furthermore," Andersen went on, "Miss Rankin has shown me her deed to the R Bar R. There is no doubt that she is the true owner."

I saw Fink brush back his coat so it wouldn't interfere with his draw. Next to him Cassidy moved sideways away from him two short steps.

The banker wasn't blind. "See here," he said, "I won't have any trouble in here."

"Stay out of this if you don't want to get hurt," Fink told him. "All you have to do is have the money ready."

He looked at me. "I've had it with you, Tackett. You've messed in my business all you're going to. Those cows are mine by rights and that money is mine, too. And I'm going to have it."

Almost casually, without taking his eyes off of me, he said, "Jump, you take the other one."

And went for his gun.

Oh, he was fast. As I went for mine I knew I wasn't going to beat him. But I knew also I was going to get off at least one shot and I was going to be careful where I aimed. He might kill me but he wasn't going to be around to hurt Esme anymore.

In a split second the room was filled with the flash and roar of guns. His first shot hit me in the left shoulder and knocked me backwards, but by this time my gun was up and I taken careful aim. His next shot, because I was stumbling back, just grazed me, but it threw my aim off enough so my shot hit him in the right arm. He reached over and took his gun with his left hand and fired wildly at me and missed.

I steadied myself and shot again and hit him in the right chest. It didn't faze him. He pumped two more shots at me, one hitting me in the right side and the other in my right shoulder. I felt myself falling. As I hit the floor another bullet hit me on the top of my left shoulder. I could hardly see now and I knew it wouldn't be long until I lost consciousness. I struggled to bring my gun up for one last shot and saw Fink taking dead aim at me. Then his hammer clicked on empty. I fought to gather enough strength to pull the trigger on my own gun and felt it go off just as I faded out of consciousness. My last thought was that I'd lost.

CHAPTER 14

SOMETHING WET and warm and raspy going back and forth across my cheek wakened me. With my eyes still shut I put a hand up to push it away and felt a warm, hairy muzzle and then a cold nose. I opened my eyes.

"Beauty, what're you doin' here?" I asked in wonderment.

Looking up, I saw a white-painted wooden ceiling. I tried to raise my head to look around, but I wasn't strong enough to lift it off the pillow. I sank back and trailed off to sleep, too tired and weak to care where I was.

I don't know how long I slept, but when I next awoke it was to the touch of a cool hand on my forehead.

"Esme?" I said faintly, not wanting to open my eyes.

"Yes, Del," she said. "It's me. You're going to be all right now."

I was weak and I wasn't thinking clearly.

"I love you," I heard myself say. In the back of my head I knowed I shouldn't have said it but at the time it seemed like the right thing to say and it sounded good when I did.

I heard her say, "I love you, too, Del." And I felt warm lips for just an instant touch mine.

"What happened?" I asked. "Where am I?"

The questions sounded familiar, like I'd asked them once before. Then it came to me. I'd been shot up in the hidden valley and I'd just managed to make it back to the ranch, or almost back, and Beauty had found me. I shook my head. That didn't seem right neither.

"What is it, Del?" Esme asked.

"Don't nothin' seem to make much sense," I said.

"You rest, my darling," she said. "I'll bring some soup in a little while."

She walked out and closed the door, but I wasn't alone. There was a gentle snore coming from the foot of the bed.

"Beauty?" I said.

The snoring stopped and I heard the soft thump of her tail hitting the spread.

I gave a sudden start. What was it I'd said? That I loved her? And she'd said she loved me. And she called me, "My darling." Now why would she do that? And why would I have said what I said? It was too much for me and I dropped off to sleep again.

It was dark when Esme awakened me. But she'd lit a couple of lamps and they gave the room a soft warm light. She'd brought in some hot beef broth and she propped a pillow under my head and began spooning the soup into my mouth. It tasted good. But it wasn't long before I shook my head "no more." I was hungry but I didn't seem to have much room in my stomach. Even so, it was just a few minutes before I felt some strength flowing through my muscles, almost like I was alive again.

"Sorry, but I don't know why I'm here," I said. "Last I remember we was down in Chambers tryin' to get yer cattle back."

"You don't remember the fight at the bank?" she asked.

I shook my head no.

"You killed Reggie Fink," she said. "But he almost killed you. Like Lew says, he shot you to doll rags."

"Yeah," I said slowly, "now it's beginnin' to come back. But I don't remember killin' him. He outdrawed me and I figured I was a goner."

"You almost were," she said. "He shot you four times, but you shot him, too, and the last time it was right through the heart. At least that's what Doc Dickery said.

"He was wonderful, too. He patched you up and Lew and Jump Cassidy. He said you should have died from shock and loss of blood. He said it's a miracle you were still alive by the time he got to you.

"He's a dear, sweet man. Between us we watched over you day and night for a week. Finally he said we could bring you back to the ranch if we took it slow and easy. So we put you in a covered wagon and brought you here and that dear man came with us to make sure you were all right and didn't begin to bleed again. He only left yesterday because he said there was nothing more he could do. Either you would make it or you wouldn't."

"How long has it been?" I asked.

"It was two weeks yesterday," she said.

Two weeks! I shook my head in disbelief. "You better tell me about the fight from the beginnin'," I said.

As she talked, it began coming back. I remembered going into the bank, the argument over the herd and the money, and finally Fink telling Jump Cassidy to take care of Lew and at the same time going for his gun. Now I remembered. His gun coming up, the smash of the first bullet and the burn of the second one before I could get my first shot off. I remembered sprawling on the floor and watching Fink take dead aim at me and his gun clicking on empty. But I couldn't remember taking my last shot at him, the shot that killed him.

Lew and Cassidy had shot each other, Esme said. Lew had been shot in the thigh and Cassidy in the side. Before they could do any more damage the banker, Bofa Levy, had jumped in. Cassidy had dropped his gun, and Levy had grabbed it off the floor, pointed it at Lew and told him to drop his gun, too, or he'd kill him. He meant it and Lew knew it so he had shoved his gun back in its holster.

It turned out that Levy wasn't no amateur. He had enlisted and fought through three years of the Civil War on the side of the North. A Jew, he had viewed the Confederate vice president, Judah P. Benjamin, as a traitor to both the nation and his religion, and had determined to atone for what he thought were

Benjamin's sins. After the war he came West where he'd fought Indians and outlaws before word came that his father had died leaving him a wealthy man. He'd refused to go back East where life would be safe and easy, instead coming to Chambers and opening the bank. This was his first taste of violence since and he'd seemed to relish it.

After disarming Lew and Cassidy he'd told Irene to get out of town or he'd see that her head was shaved and that she'd be tarred and feathered and ridden out on a rail. Oh, he was one tough hombre, even if he was a banker. As Irene started to go, she took off the gold chain with the locket on it and threw it at Esme.

"Take your damned locket," she screamed. "It's nothing but bad luck."

By this time Marshal Simpson and Doc Dickery had arrived. The banker and Andersen, who'd pushed Esme aside and sheltered her with his body during the shooting, told the marshal what had happened. Without hesitation he'd escorted Irene to a Santa Fe-bound stage that was just leaving town and had put her on it without even giving her time to get her clothes.

Lew and Cassidy were both out and around by the end of the week and Simpson had also ordered Cassidy out of town as a troublemaker.

"He told Mr. Cassidy that he could leave or go to jail and face trial for attempted murder," Esme said. "Mr. Cassidy chose to leave. He said to tell you that if you lived he held no grudge. He said you were 'a real fighting man' and that he hoped you'd make it."

Just talking had tired me out and by the time Esme had finished telling me about Cassidy I was falling asleep again.

When morning came I was feeling stronger and I felt gingerly around to see where I'd been wounded. It seemed like everywhere I felt there was a bandage. There were no bandages on my head, but the raw scar from being shot in the hidden valley still tingled when I touched it. I rubbed my hand down my cheek and stopped short. I'd been unconscious for two weeks but my face felt like I

170

had no more than a day's growth of beard. Someone had shaved me. Who? And now that I thought about it I was wearing a night-shirt. Someone had undressed me and got me into it. Who?

Whilst I was trying to figure that out, there was a knock on the door and Mary Lou came in carrying a tray. On it was something that looked like cornmeal mush—and later tasted like it—and toast and a mug of steaming hot coffee. All at once I was real hungry. Mary Lou said a cheery "good morning" and asked how I felt.

"Fine," I said. "Rarin' to go."

She set the tray down, put an extra pillow under my head, and began spooning out the mush. I pushed her hand away.

"I can feed myself," I protested.

But when I tried I found I couldn't hold the spoon steady.

"You win," I said.

"Who's been takin' care of me?" I asked between bites.

"Esme, mostly," Mary Lou answered. "She wanted to. But we've all helped. If we had to turn you or clean you up Blackie or Jack came in."

Just then Beauty trotted in. "Beauty helped, too," Mary Lou said. "She's slept in here with you every night."

She was just leaving when Esme came in. Her black hair, hit by a stray ray of sunshine, gave off a dark reddish glow. She looked a little thinner than I remembered and I put it down to all that had gone on. She sat on the edge of the bed and took my hand.

"I been a lot of trouble," I said.

"You saved my ranch and my cattle and probably my life," she said. "There's no way I can ever thank you."

"No need," I said gruffly. "Told you when I come to work that I ride for the brand."

"You also told me you were a cowboy and not a gunfighter," she reminded, "but you fought with one of the most dangerous men in the west on my behalf."

I changed the subject. "Soon as I'm well enough to ride, 'bout a week, I figure, I'll be driftin'."

Her face fell and I could see that she was fighting back tears. That had been a dumb thing for me to say.

"I'll hang around awhile 'til I get my strength back," I amended.

She began, "Last night you said . . ." when I interrupted.

"Shouldn't have said it. Didn't have no right to."

She tucked my hand back beneath the covers and forced a smile.

"We'll talk about it when you're stronger. The boys have asked if they can come in and I told them if you were up to it they could see you for just a few minutes."

After a bit they trooped in. Lew was walking with a limp but I noticed that Sears had his hand out of the sling and was using it without any trouble.

He was the first to speak. "Thought I was gonna lose ya," he said, but there was no anger or hatred in his voice, just a trace of humor.

"I'm too mean to die," I said. "Remember that."

After they asked how I felt and I said fine, they stood around awkwardly for a minute or two, not knowing what else to say, then Lew and Blackie said they see me later and left. Sears came over and looked down at me.

"Yer a good man, Tackett," he said. "Ifn it's all right with you I'd kind of like to let bygones be bygones."

"I'd like that," I said. "You saved my life. No way I could fight you."

I pulled my hand from beneath the covers and with an effort stuck it out. He took it in his own rough, calloused hand and shook it.

"Deal," he said. Then he laughed. "Someday when I know yer well, I'm gonna fist fight you just for fun. I wanna see how good you are when you don't sneak the first punch."

"Deal," I said.

A week had nearly passed before I felt up to trying to get out of bed. But for the last few days I'd managed to sit up and shave and

172

wash myself. With the help of Sears and Blackie I finally was able to take a few halting steps to a chair and in another two days I was moving around slow and carefully by myself, with just the aid of a cane.

On a warm evening near the end of June I walked carefully out on the veranda that ran along the front of the house and sat down in one of the wooden chairs. It was good to be outside, breathing the scents of the cattle and horses and the desert sagebrush that were carried on a slight breeze that was blowing in from the desert.

Beauty, who'd been wandering around in the ranch yard, came and lay down at my feet. In a few minutes Esme came out the front door and sat down in the chair next to me.

I knew there was something on her mind—her and me, most likely—and I wasn't ready to talk about us yet. We'd both been avoiding the subject ever since the day I'd told her I'd be moving along. And I wanted to keep avoiding it for a while longer.

"Ma's diary," I said. "Did you bring it back to the ranch with us?"

"Yes," she said. "It's in the house in a safe place."

"Thanks," I said.

We sat there quietly for a while. Then she ventured, "I could read it for you."

I felt my face redden and the old feeling of shame at not being able to read came over me.

"It's somethin' I got to do myself," I said.

"Del," she said, reaching out and taking my hand. "I know you don't read very well, but I could teach you. You're smart. You could learn in a hurry."

"It's somethin' I got to learn for myself," I said.

"You are a stubborn man, Del Tackett," she said, standing up. "Why won't you let me help?"

I just shook my head. "I got to do it myself," I repeated.

"Men!" she snapped, and turned and stomped inside, slamming the door behind her.

I sat there feeling miserable and sorry for myself. I couldn't tell her why I wouldn't let her help me because I wasn't sure I really knew, myself. In the back of my mind, I guess, I thought it was a man's place to help a woman and not the other way around. I didn't want her looking down on me or feeling sorry for me or thinking she had to take me by the hand and teach me or lead me. How could she ever look up to me if she had to teach me how to read and write and do sums like any schoolboy?

I knew then what I was going to do. As soon as I was strong enough I was going to leave and I was going to find a way to get me some sort of education. Then I would come back here, if I still felt like I wanted to, and see if Esme would have me if she hadn't married someone else by then.

But I knew I was just kidding myself about that last part. You can't go off and leave a pretty girl and have her moping around a year or two waiting for you. Sure as apple pie, some other feller is going to come along and make her forget all about you. I guessed it was a chance I would have to take.

The next morning at breakfast Esme didn't have much to say and when she talked it was to anyone but me. After the boys had finished up and headed out I sat there drinking a third mug of coffee. Esme left the room for a minute, then came back carrying the diary. She handed it to me and then ran from the room without saying a word, which made me feel even worse than I'd already been feeling.

I left the house and went down to the corral and whistled for Old Dobbin. He came over and nuzzled me

"We'll be movin' on in a few days," I said.

I went to the barn and found my saddle and discovered I was strong enough to lift it. It won't be long now, I thought to myself.

At midday Jack Sears came riding in. He'd been gone for almost a week. He came and sat down beside me on the veranda.

"Been down to Tucson checkin' on the Lazy A," he said. "Ain't no deed on file for it, which I thought maybe would be the case. So I filed my own deed. Mary Lou and I been thinking about maybe gettin' married and movin' in there. I think we can make a go of it. Be good for you and Esme to have neighbors."

"Be good for Esme," I said. "I'll be moving along in a day or two. I'm happy for you and Mary Lou. She'll make you a good wife."

"Yeah and I'm gonna do my damndest to make her a good husband," Jack said. "Time I was settlin' down."

Another wave of loneliness swept over me. Why was I such a damn fool? Why didn't I stay and let Esme teach me to read? For that matter, why didn't I stay and marry her? She'd have me. I knew it.

Dang! I knew I had to get out of here and away before I did something dumb like changing my mind.

I got up and went inside, looking for Esme. I found her at the big desk in the living room working on ranch accounts. She looked up when I came in, but didn't smile.

"I'll be leavin' in the mornin'," I said.

"You're welcome to stay," she said, but there was no warmth in her voice.

"I better not," I said.

"I owe you two months pay," she said. "That will be eighty dollars. Foreman's pay."

She got up and went over to the picture of her mother, swung it to one side and dialed open the safe. She took out four double eagles and handed them to me. I put them in my pocket and we stood there looking at each other, not saying anything. Finally she turned away and went back to the desk.

"Come back anytime, Del," she said. "I owe you a great deal and you'll always be welcome."

I went on into the kitchen to find Mary Lou. She and Sears were sitting at the big table having coffee.

"You and Jack'll make a fine pair. Name one of the kids after me, huh?"

She blushed and smiled. "We'll miss you, Del. Won't we, Jack."

He nodded. "Come by the ranch anytime. You'll always be welcome."

Lew and Blackie rode in at sundown and at dinner I announced to them that I'd be leaving. That kind of put a damper on the table talk and we pretty much ate in silence. After dinner I went to the bedroom, bundled up my things and taken them out to the bunkhouse, where I slept for the first time since the shooting.

Just like before, I was up at dawn. After I washed up I packed my gear, threw my saddle on Old Dobbin, along with my bedroll, and headed for the kitchen for breakfast. I was the first to finish.

Standing up, I said, "Well, I guess it's time I was goin'."

I looked around at them. We'd been through a lot together in not a very long time. And we'd become friends. More like family than friends, I thought. First family I'd had since I left Ma more than twelve years ago.

Suddenly, I didn't want to go. But I'd made my choice. I went over and took my hat off the peg by the door. I turned back to the table to say a final "So long" and almost bumped into Esme. Standing on her tiptoes she reached up and pulled my head down and kissed me firmly on the lips.

"Good bye, Del," she whispered "Come back."

I straightened up and looked one more time at my friends. "So long," I said and went out.

Outside Beauty was worrying a large beef bone. I went over and patted her head.

"So long, Beauty," I said softly.

She left off gnawing the bone long enough to wag her tail and lick my hand. I was going to miss her, too. I'd never had a dog for a pet and she was more than a pet. Like the folks inside she was family.

I mounted old Dobbin and gave him his head. He hadn't been ridden much since the shooting and he was eager to go. Without thinking we headed south at a fast trot and three hours later we were on the north edge of Nora.

The sight of Nora Wetstone's place of business jogged my memory. I'd meant to come back and lay down some law to her. I'd not forgotten or forgiven how she'd treated Esme, even if she had done it for her badman son, Reggie Fink, alias Ray Failor. Dismounting in front of the big adobe house, I tied Old Dobbin to the hitching post and went up and knocked on the door. A buxom young woman with old eyes and brown hair opened it and invited me in.

"I didn't come for fun, I come to see Nora," I said.

"She's not here anymore. She's gone," the woman said. "I'm the owner now. She sold out to me a month ago."

"Where'd she go?" I asked.

"Santa Fe, I think. There was a big shooting down at Chambers a while back and shortly after that she got a letter from Santa Fe. Right away she said she was leaving for good, said she'd sell me the building for whatever I could scrape up. I'd saved a little money and she took it and deeded the place over to me and the next day her and that Mexican woman hitched the team to the buckboard and drove off. I ain't seen them since."

"Thanks, miss," I said. "That answers my questions."

"Are you sure you won't stay?" she asked almost wistfully.

I smiled at her. "Another time, maybe," I said.

I hadn't yet got my strength back and I was tired from the long ride, and hungry, too. From Nora's I rode to the saloon, meaning to get a beer and go across the road for lunch at the little cafe. Afterward, I'd ride 'til I was tired, then find a place to camp for the night. It had been a while since I'd slept under the stars and I was looking forward to shedding that cooped-up feeling too many nights in the house had brought on.

Dismounting from Old Dobbin I tied him next to half a dozen other horses at the hitch rail, and strolled through the batwing doors and into the saloon. When my eyes got used to the dimness I seen five men standing at the bar drinking. Four of them were taller than me and the shortest one was bigger in the shoulders than any of them. He was all muscle and a yard wide. Looking over his shoulder the short one seen me and nudged the man next to him. He said something but I didn't catch it.

They turned as one man and looked at me. They were big men, wide in the shoulders and narrow in the hips. Their wedge-shaped faces were weatherbeaten and tough looking. All but one were wearing range clothes and that one was wearing a broadcloth suit, a white shirt, and a string tie but, like the others, he was wearing a gun low on his hip and tied down. He kind of squinted at me a moment, then he grinned.

"Howdy, stranger," he said. "Meanin' no offense, would you be kind enough to tell me your name?"

Well, why not, I thought. I wasn't ashamed of my name. Besides these five fellers could beat it out of me if they wanted to.

I grinned back. "Tackett," I said. "Del Tackett."

"I thought as much," he said. "You don't look like kinfolk."

He downed his drink and the others followed suit. Then, one after the other, they filed past me and out the door. In a moment I heard the sound of their horses fading in the distance.

I went on up to the bar and told the skinny bartender I wanted a beer.

"What was that all about?" I asked.

"Danged if I know," he said. "They come in to Nora couple of days ago. Said they heard some feller name of Sackett might be trouble around here and they were come to help. Must have been you they meant. I guess they decided not to stay around once they found your name was Tackett instead of Sackett."

So those were the Sacketts.

They'd come to help a kinsman in trouble. Only thing was, I wasn't no kinsman. That familiar wave of loneliness swept over me again. I hadn't any kinfolk by any name that I knew of. Ever since I was sixteen I'd lived my life and fought my fights all by myself. I studied myself in the mirror behind the bar. A big, rough-looking man with a knife scar on his left cheeck and hair coming in white where that bullet had creased my skull. Those men who'd just left weren't no beauties, but neither was I. Difference was, they had each other and I was all alone.

Just then I felt a tap on my shoulder. I turned to see another man who was nearly a dead ringer for the tall men who'd just left.

"I was sittin' over in the corner when you come in," he said. "Them was my kinfolk, cousins and such. I love 'em but sometimes I just need to get away from 'em so I let 'em go.

"I heard you say yer name was Tackett. Them was Sacketts, in case you didn't know it. They left because you ain't kin and you don't look like you was in trouble."

He put a hand on my shoulder. "Friend, the Sacketts are mostly from the Tennessee hills. They're a mighty clannish lot. Me, I ain't from there. My great, great grandfather went north and settled in the piney woods along the New Jersey coast and that's where I'm from. But I been out here near twenty-five years now, ever since the war. Name is Hacken Sackett. If you need a friend sometime send the word and I'll come. My kinfolk up in Mora'll get word to me. I figure anyone named Tackett has got to have some Sackett in him somewhere.

"See you around."

He turned down the offer of another drink and left. I was sorry to see him go, him being friendly and all. But as he rode off I thought, I got friends, after all. I got friends—family almost—back at the R Bar R. And now one of them Sacketts is a friend, too. Not too bad.

I swallowed down the last of my beer, paid up, and headed for the little cafe across the road. I'd have a meal and then head out. As I walked it come to me where I was going. There was a big, wide world out there, things to do, people to meet. There was a school teacher down in Abilene and one day I was going to look her up. I wanted to find her and tell her about her daddy, old Billy Bob Doyle. And maybe she was the one who could teach me to read.

Then I paused right there in the middle of the street. An hour ago I'd been eager to go find her but now, for some reason, that didn't seem so important. Maybe finding her could wait a while. It occurred to me that it was seeing the Sacketts that changed my mind. In that few minutes in the saloon they'd taught me something. Not about guns or gun fighting, but about family.

Except for Ma I'd never had a family. But, come to think about it, back there at the R Bar R, I did have family waiting for me. Not blood kinfolk, maybe, but family nevertheless, like I'd never had before. No matter what I did or where I went I knew in my heart they'd always be there and would always welcome me home.

And among them was a girl, a special kind of girl that one day, after I'd learned to read and after I'd found out what was in that diary Ma had left, I hoped I could ask to marry me.

Suddenly, I wanted to see her real bad. And the rest of them, too. Jack Sears, Lew and Blackie and Mary Lou. I turned in midstride and strode, almost ran, to where Old Dobbin was tied. In a second I was in the saddle, and Old Dobbin, like he knew we were going home, was off and running.

Coming Soom

TACKETT
& THE TEACHER

TACKETT
2
TRILOGY